Arepo
Cure of Souls Series
Book One

By W. W. Whitten

AREPO

Cover designed by Jeremy Savard

Cover art:
Copyright Shutterstock 50349574
Copyright Shutterstock 126058712
Copyright Shutterstock 166016213

Published by W. W. Whitten
Prtined by Lightning Source

Visit the author website:
www.wwwhitten.com

ISBN: 978-0-9968158-0-2 (Paperback)

Version 2015.09.14

Printed in the United States of America

10 9 8 7 6 5 4 3 2 1

Acknowledgments

I never believed in magic until I wrote this book, or rather until I met my editor, Marge Lee. Her talents verge on the supernatural. She has the ability to mimic my writing style in such a way that I'm unable to tell where my words began and her edits finished. Thank you, Marge. Brilliant!

Pastor Tom Hartley and Rabbi Jeff Goldwasser were invaluable for the research necessary to complete this novel. Thank you, Gentlemen.

Jeremy Savard's cover art could sell a block of bound blank pages. Books *are* judged by their covers; thanks, Jeremy, for creating the perfect first impression for this book.

Kelly J. Pfeiffer introduced me to the Kübler-Ross model of grief and the Bonanno, Corr, and McDougall studies of the same subject. Thanks for letting me pick your brain.

Dr. Teresa Burns's work with Renaissance Hermeticism, especially her article on the Folger Museum's Book of Magic, helped me better understand an interesting period of European history.

Finally, I am grateful to the Folger Museum for digitizing its grimoire (MS. V.b.26). For someone who spends most of his time within the same four walls, a searchable database of digitized material is priceless.

Chapter 1

New York, New York

Sotheby's Auction House

Julian Thomas stood at the back of the room and watched the drama unfold.

A highly publicized, illuminated manuscript from 1465 was projected onto two screens flanking the auctioneer. Its images showed Pontius Pilate, convicted for his crimes against Jesus Christ, standing trial in chains before Emperor Tiberius. The scenes were from a play, *Mystére de la Vengeance*, by Eustache Maracadé.

In the auction house's crowded room, necks craned to peer around cellphones held aloft to capture the sale on video.

"Sir, may I take your coat?"

"No." Julian recoiled from the auction attendant and tightly clutched the frayed lapels of his wool coat.

"Very well, Sir. On which lot are you bidding?"

"Lot 22."

The attendant nodded. "Once this lot has sold, seats should open up front. Lot 22 is next. Good luck."

The bidding on Lot 21, the medieval manuscript, began at $4.5 million. The room was abuzz, but only three parties remained after the frenetic bidding reached six million. The final bidder won the auction to much fanfare. The applause died, whispers circulated that the prize belonged to the Getty Museum, and the chairs began to empty.

Julian nervously patted the right pocket of his coat.

He subconsciously traced the outline in his pocket and prayed his sacrifice would be rewarded and his sins forgiven. He removed his coat, adjusted it so the weighted pocket was nestled in his lap, and settled into an aisle chair in the seventh row.

Lot 22 would not draw the attention the medieval manuscript had just demanded. Still, Julian worried about the well-dressed, and probably well-funded, groups in the first three rows of chairs.

He had scraped together all he could but still fell short of the anticipated auction price of $25,000 to $35,000. So, he broke yet another commandment. *Thou shall not steal.* He had slipped into his church's office during the Wednesday evening service, when staffing was limited, and walked out with $13,000 from its coffers.

His guilt and the $37,274 in his pocket burned like brimstone in his belly.

A new auctioneer took the podium, and the two bordering screens again sprang to life. Lot 22 was displayed brilliantly to the now nearly empty auction gallery. The lot was listed as fourteen manuscript pages from a sixteenth-century grimoire, or book of magic.

The well-dressed groups in the front of the room shared whispers and stiffened in their straight-backed chairs. Julian dug his fingers into the wool on his lap.

The auctioneer began.

"Lot 22 is a wonderful collection of spells, conjurations, and maledictions. The fourteen pages are in good condition, with light stippling and some discoloration. But, they are a fine example of the occult phenomenon that took hold of sixteenth- and seventeenth-century Europe."

"I'd like to start the bidding at $15,000."

Julian smiled. The starting price was lower than he expected. Maybe he could purchase the pages and still make amends with his church.

He thought about the lot number of the grimoire pages. In Biblical studies, 22 is a significant number. Each of the three cycles of the Canon Wheel—Genesis through Songs of Solomon, Isaiah through Acts, and Romans through Revelations—includes 22 books. And, there are 22 letters in the Hebrew alphabet. Jesus's death followed Abraham's birth by exactly 2,200 years. Julian hoped this meant that providence was on his side.

His smile faded when the people in the first three rows raised their paddles nearly in unison.

"Thank you," the auctioneer said. "I have $15,000. Do I have $16,000?

Again the paddles rose quickly.

"Now $16,000, do I have $17,000?"

All paddles went up without hesitation.

"Very well. Do I have $20,000?"

The three groups now settled into a rhythm.

"Twenty-one thousand? Thank you."

The auctioneer indicated the woman sitting in the front row and flanked by two distinguished-looking men.

"I now have $21,000, do I have $22,000?"

The group in the third row shook their heads.

"I have $21,000, is there a bid of $22,000?"

Julian bit his lip and prayed for patience. He did not want to tip his hat too soon. He stayed his hand, and watched the man in the second row raise his paddle.

"Twenty-two thousand now, from the gentleman."

The auctioneer looked to the woman up front. "Madame, will you bid $23,000?"

She nodded.

"Excellent. Sir, do I have $24,000?"

"Twenty-five thousand dollars!" the man declared.

Just like that, Julian's hope of repaying the church vanished. He breathed deeply and dropped his head, but his eyes darted up when the woman in the first row immediately responded.

"Twenty-seven!"

"Very good," the auctioneer replied. "I now have $27,000 with the lady in the first row. The bid is with you, Sir?"

The man turned to the companion on his right and whispered. Dejected, he turned back to the auctioneer and shook his head.

"Very well, then. Still at $27,000. Are there any further bids in the room?"

Julian saw the woman in the front row turn with a beaming smile to her compatriots.

"I have $27,000 going once . . ."

"Thirty thousand dollars." Julian raised his paddle.

The woman and her two friends pivoted in their chairs. Her smile had vanished. Several standing bystanders took seats in the gallery.

"Ah, we have a new bidder. Thank you, Sir." The auctioneer smiled. "I have $30,000 now for the book of magic. Do I have another bid?"

He scanned the room, but his eyes knowingly fell on the trio in the front row.

They huddled and whispered. They glanced at Julian more than once.

"Madame, do you have a bid?" the auctioneer prompted. He now left the question open-ended so as not to repress the price.

The trio broke its huddle, and the woman spoke.

"Thirty-five thousand dollars!"

Julian felt the blood drain from his face. His breath rattled. He scrubbed his sweaty palms on the wool in his lap.

"Sir, I have $35,000. The bid is yours."

"Thirty-seven thousand five hundred dollars!" Julian gulped inwardly. Surely Sotheby's would forgive a minor $226 discrepancy.

The trio again spun to gape at him.

"Thank you. I have $37,500. Madame?"

The trio frantically strategized. Julian bent his head and silently prayed.

"I have $37,500 from the gentleman in the middle of the room. Are there any further bids?"

The trio of bidders continued to huddle.

"Thirty-seven thousand five hundred dollars, going once."

Julian smiled and slowly raised his head.

"Thirty-seven thousand five hundred dollars, going twice."

Still silence.

"If there are no further bids, I will conclude the sale at $37,500."

Julian straightened, raised his eyes to Heaven, and thanked the Lord.

"Very well, then. The textbook of magic is sold for . . ."

"Forty thousand dollars!" the lady in the front row cried out.

The gallery gasped. Julian's face slackened. His mouth fell open. Forty, the number of completion and fulfillment in the Bible.

"I now have $40,000. Sir, the bid is yours."

The auctioneer looked to Julian, as did the trio up front.

Julian could not respond. His mouth worked up and down, but no words took shape. The auctioneer closed his eyes and nodded.

"I have $40,000 going once." He scanned the room, but his eyes never again met Julian's.

"Forty thousand dollars, going twice."

The auctioneer lifted the gavel.

"That's $40,000 for the book of magic, sold to the lady in the front row." The gavel fell.

As the gallery broke into applause, the clack of wood against wood brought tears to Julian's eyes. He watched the trio in the front celebrate and accept congratulations. The woman's face was triumphant. Julian overheard a name.

Folger.

Of course. The Folger Shakespeare Museum. It owned the remaining portion of the grimoire.

As Julian rose from his chair, so did his spirits. The pages would not disappear into a private collection. His lips moved silently, muttering a prayer, as he shrugged into his coat. He could return the money to his church, and there may still be a chance to put his hands on Lot 22.

That is, if he lived long enough to do so.

Chapter 2

Denver, Colorado

Detective Oren Pope pulled his unmarked, city-owned Ford Inter-ceptor Utility vehicle to the curb of Emporia Court in northeast Denver. The uniforms had the street cordoned off, and the CSU team was being debriefed outside the victim's front door. His part-ner's car was down the block, but Pope did not see Max within the huddled crowd in front of the victim's house. The detective opened his glove box and removed a container of Vicks VapoRub. He opened it and then dabbed some of the ointment in each nostril. Max had already warned him about the condition of the body.

Pope slipped out of the sedan and tugged on some latex gloves as he made his way up the walk. He skirted the CSU team and showed his gold badge to the young uniformed officer at the door.

"Is Detective Prebys inside?" Pope asked.

"Yes, Sir."

"Looks like you got lucky today. At least you get some fresh air," Pope added.

"I was inside earlier. I can still smell it."

"It'll take weeks before those particles of rotting flesh dislodge themselves from your olfactory nodes."

"Weeks?"

"You're lucky it wasn't a floater, or a burner."

The young officer stuck his head outside and breathed deeply.

Pope drifted toward the voices and the odor coming from the back of the house. *So much for the Vicks.*

He keenly assessed his surroundings. The victim's house was well-appointed and neatly organized. It was nice, just as he expected, considering the neighborhood. The surfaces and the corners were clean. A pen rested parallel to a small tablet of paper beside a telephone. A DVD and CD collection stood alphabetized on the shelves of an entertainment center. Small pillows sat in a perfect line across the sofa. It felt too clean, sterile. Something was missing.

"Hey, Partner." Max Prebys stood near the body in the center of the kitchen floor.

"It's too clean, Max."

"Only you would walk into this cesspool and call it clean. You must live in a sty."

"Pull out the body, clean up the blood and other fluids, and you could eat off the counters," Pope said as he knelt to examine the body.

"That's a disgusting thought," Prebys muttered.

"Has the M.E. seen the body?"

Prebys nodded. "Yup. He's waiting on us to release the scene so he can take the road kill."

"Road kill? Nice." Pope shook his head.

"Come on, with the bloating, what's the first thing you think of?"

Pope had to admit his partner was right. There was an opossum on the side of the road near his house that looked very similar to poor Mr. Ellis here on his kitchen floor.

"I'm guessing about two weeks," Pope said.

"The M.E. agrees, considering the bloating and fragility of the skin."

"And, are we certain of identification?"

"As far as we can tell. Hair color and height seem to match. Wallet was in his pocket. Credits cards and ID match Addison Ellis. Finger prints won't help, but dental should put it to rest."

Pope nodded. He leaned as close as he dared to the handle of the knife protruding from Ellis's chest.

"Doc says the blade must be caught on a rib, otherwise it should have dislodged with the bloating."

"Interesting handle. Ever see anything like it?"

"Nope. Certainly not a kitchen knife."

"If it's unique, it may lead us somewhere. We should bag all the kitchen utensils for comparison," Pope suggested.

"Already been ordered."

Pope stood and looked around the kitchen.

"No sign of struggle. Forced entry?"

"Not that we can tell. Obviously, the skin's not going to help, but the doc said he'll look deeper for bruising and what not. CSU is still working the yard, windows, and doors."

"Not a robbery either," Prebys added. "Did you see the size of that TV? I don't have a wall big enough for that beast."

"I still say something feels wrong about this place. Too nice. Too clean," said Pope.

"You're right. Follow me." Prebys waved for Pope to follow.

There was a small hallway, with two adjacent rooms and a bathroom between. Pope peered into the small bedroom. It looked much like the rest of the house. Well-appointed and neatly decorated. The bathroom door was open, as well. It was small, but modern in design and perfectly clean. In spite of the decomposition clinging to everything, the smell of bleach in the small room tickled Pope's nose through the Vicks.

"In there." Prebys pointed to the third room. "Take note of the steel door and deadbolt. It locks from the outside."

"To keep someone in, not out," Pope agreed.

Pope stepped into the small room. It would have been a boy's paradise. There were gaming consoles of every make and model, with hundreds of accompanying games, attached to another beast of a television. Toys and board games lined shelves running the length of the room, and there was a partially completed model of an aircraft carrier on a table in a corner.

"Did this guy have a kid?" Pope asked.

"Not as far as we can tell. Not married. Bedroom closet and dresser hold clothes for one."

"Maybe he had partial custody," Pope suggested.

"Maybe."

"I just realized this place has no pictures. Nothing on the wall. Nothing beside the bed."

Prebys looked around. "You're right. It kind of looks like it's staged. Maybe he was selling. Real estate agents tell you to pull out the personal touches. That way, prospective buyers can picture themselves in the home."

"Maybe. Let's see if it's on the market." Pope crossed the room. "Obviously, we'll need all this stuff fingerprinted." Pope revolved slowly in a tight circle in the middle of the room.

"There should be a window in here. Front of the house. I'm certain two windows can be seen from the street."

Pope shook his head. "Something is very wrong here, Max."

Chapter 3

New York, New York

Julian shifted on the leather chair in the lobby of the Park Hyatt Hotel so that he could watch the front door.

He had been there for nearly two hours and was concerned about the attention he was attracting from hotel security. He again shuffled his research papers on the low table in front of him, in an attempt to exude an image of belonging. He often checked his watch and shook his head, as if he was on stage and playing the part of an impatient businessman.

Julian had called several hotels in the midtown area in search of the Folger Shakespeare staff. He identified the names of the auction trio from pictures on the Folger's website and began asking for them at the reservation desks of hotels in a seven-block area. He found their reservations under the name of Ms. Erica Lyall, who was, according to the website, the Folger's manuscript curator.

At the auction, Julian had learned that the winning bidder could take ownership of Lot 22 three days after the close of the auction. He had bet on the fact that Ms. Lyall would stay in New York to personally claim and transport the piece, as opposed to having it shipped to the Folger in Washington, D.C. According to the Hyatt employee, his gamble had paid off. Ms. Lyall had returned Julian's call last evening, and she agreed to meet him in the hotel lobby at 6:00 p.m.

Julian checked his watch again. It was 7:53 p.m. She was nearly two hours late.

"Dr. Thomas?"

Julian looked up to see Erica Lyall approaching briskly. He stood and felt the weight of the item in his right pocket. He reassuringly patted the pocket before extending his hand to Dr. Lyall.

"I'm sorry I'm so late. I'm glad you waited." She shook his hand warmly.

Her smile was genuine.

"I'm just happy you chose to meet with me, Dr. Lyall."

"Please call me Erica. Shall we sit?"

"Here?" Julian looked around the lobby.

"Is this not okay?"

"It's just that . . . well, my . . . I mean, our conversation might attract some unwanted attention."

"Is that right?" Erica's smile slipped a bit. "Then perhaps this should wait until I get back to D.C. You could schedule an appointment."

"My, my, no. I thought maybe we could just find a quieter corner for our discussion."

"I've found it much easier to disappear in a crowd. Join me in the bar?" Erica turned and started across the lobby, her heels clicking on the marble tile.

Julian began to follow, but suddenly remembered his papers strewn on the table. He quickly gathered them and then hurried after the curator. He caught up to her as she leaned across the bar and ordered her drink.

"Could I get you something?" she asked.

"Uh, no. Thank you."

Erica shrugged. She accepted the glass of wine from the bartender and nodded toward the only empty table in the busy space. They each sat in the low chairs. Erica crossed her legs, removed her right shoe, and rubbed her foot.

"So, you're a doctor of religious studies and philosophy. Where did you get your degrees?" Erica asked over the din of bar conversation.

"Wheaton College."

"Wheaton? Illinois?"

"Yes."

"Excellent school. Stellar reputation." Erica sipped her wine and nodded her approval. "You had me sweating at the auction, Dr. Thomas. I'm not sure I would have received approval for another bid."

"I only wish I'd had enough money for another bid," said Julian.

"Well, Doctor, you said the grimoire pages are critical to your study of the Society of Mercurii. I'm intrigued."

"You're familiar with the Mercurii? Good. So, you know that your grimoire was in their possession?"

She nodded.

"As far as we can tell. It was, after all, a secret magical society," she chuckled.

"But," she continued, "we *know* the grimoire was in the possession of R. C. Smith and John Palmer."

"Correct," affirmed Julian. Both also were suspected members of the Society of Mercurii."

Julian now leaned closer to the curator.

"I believe your book of magic also once belonged to the English portrait-painter Richard Cosway, and I believe he was a founding member of the Mercurii, as well."

"You're not the first to propose that theory."

"No, of course not. But, do you know of the Bateleur cipher?"

Now Erica leaned forward. "Bateleur?"

"You don't know of the Bateleur or *Il Bagatto* tarot card?"

"I am the manuscript curator at a Shakespeare library, which just happens to have a grimoire in its collection. I don't have time for such nonsense," Erica bristled.

"Of course, sorry. The Bateleur, or Magician, is one of the trump cards in the tarot deck. He is of specific significance in the Tarot de Marseille deck. He is clever and a master of both the physical and spiritual realms."

"And you believe there is a cipher pertaining to Bateleur in the pages I've just procured?" asked Erica.

"I do," responded Julian.

"What's the significance of the cipher?"

"I don't know," Julian lied. "That's why I need to see the pages."

"Not a problem." Erica smiled. "Once the conservator has finished with the pages, I would welcome your visit to the Folger."

"Thank you, but I was hoping to see the pages tonight."

Erica recoiled.

"Tonight? Heavens, no. Under what conditions? My hotel room? Absolutely not."

Julian flipped quickly through his stack of papers until he came to a copy of page 135 of the book of magic which the Folger already owned.

He placed it in front of the curator.

"You'll recognize this, of course."

"The John Porter cipher," she said, after a quick glance at the page.

"It is a cipher, but its solution is not John Porter," said Julian as he rubbed his temples.

"What? Of course it is." Erica looked incredulously at Julian. "It's a simple backwards cipher."

"Too simple." Julian arched his eyebrows and loosened his tie.

"What do you mean?"

Julian pulled another sheet from his pile of research material. He laid it on the table between them.

On the sheet was a copy of the face and reverse of a tarot card. The detail of the character on the card, Le Bateleur, was exquisite. The image showed a man wearing a wide-brimmed hat and standing behind a table on which were several items.

"I understand that you are not a student of the tarot, but I assure you, this is not an ordinary tarot card.

Julian passed the sheet to the curator. "Look at the facial detail of Bateleur."

He watched her study the image.

"This card, and the deck it came from, was hand-painted by Richard Cosway."

Erica's eyes darted up from the page.

"In fact, the deck *belonged* to Cosway."

"You have this actual card?" asked Erica.

Julian nodded. "I have the *deck*, in its entirety." Julian patted his pocket once more.

"You have it *with* you? *Here?* May I see it?"

"I need to study those fourteen pages." Julian gathered his materials and stood. "Shall we?"

Erica looked up at him in disbelief. "What? You come up to my room, and I show you mine, and you show me yours?"

"Of course."

Erica stared at him.

"In fact, once I've had time to study the manuscript pages, then you may keep the tarot deck."

"That deck would be worth thousands!" Erica exclaimed.

"I bought it two years ago for $15,000," Julian responded matter-of-factly.

"You're serious." Erica shook her head in disbelief.

Julian patted his pocket once again. Then he looked at his watch.

Erica made her decision.

"Well, okay, then."

Chapter 4

Denver, Colorado

Major Crimes Division

Detective Pope sat at his desk and studied the case file.

Addison Ellis's body was positively identified by his dental records. Research into his financials, insurance, and employment history proved that Ellis was single and childless. Nor did he have a criminal record.

The autopsy showed Ellis to be in good health, aside from being dead. There was no subcutaneous bruising, so he did not fight his attacker.

There were no signs of forced entry. All windows were locked, and the locks were in good working order. Door jambs and locking mechanisms were pristine, including the oddly placed deadbolt lock on the interior steel door.

Ellis's were the only fingerprints found anywhere in the home.

Pope's thumbnail flicked the edge of a photo. He squinted at the image of the strange knife that had been removed from Ellis's chest. It was a wide, double-edged blade with a black handle. The blade was etched with an intricate scroll, and the handle was inlayed with white stones on each side. Pope was unfamiliar with the symbols depicted by the inlays.

"It's late, Partner." Max Prebys stood and pulled his coat over his jacket. "Wife won't be happy. See you in the morning."

"Max, you ever see anything like this before?" Pope turned the photo around.

"Nope." Prebys buttoned his coat and pulled a pair of gloves from the pockets.

"It looks expensive, right? So, why leave it behind? The killer obviously brought it with him."

"Maybe he couldn't tug it free," Prebys offered.

"Maybe."

Prebys pulled on his hat. "I'll see you tomorrow."

"Okay, Partner. Tell Linda, 'Hello.'"

"Not a chance. She thinks you hang the moon. One mention of your name, and I'll be compared to you all night," Prebys called over his shoulder. "No one needs that kind of pressure when he's giving it to his wife." He made a pumping gesture with his arm.

"*Giving* it? You probably have to *pay* her to take what you're offering."

Prebys extended a gloved middle finger over his shoulder.

"And who says 'hang the moon' anymore?"

"Just old farts like me. Bye, Kid."

Pope did a web search of "black-handled knife." Several kitchen-knife ads and photos of survival knives popped up. But the sites that drew his attention were those mentioning magic, Wiccans, and witches. After browsing multiple sites, Pope's search was rewarded.

The knife was called an athame, and it was used in Wiccan rituals.

However, the blade was never actually used to cut anything, according to Wiccan tradition. But, mused Pope, a blade is still a blade. And, it makes an excellent murder weapon, no matter its intended purpose.

In the margin of the file, Pope wrote "cult?" Murders never really had a cult angle to them. The perpetrator was probably some pimpled-face outcast who dressed up in robes and beat off to anime. However, *this* pimple-face was highly organized and extremely dangerous.

Pope yawned. It had been a long day. *Maybe Prebys was right. Home for dinner, even in an empty house, sounded pretty good.*

"Hey, Detective."

Pope looked up to see the young tech specialist, Tommy, approaching.

"You're gonna want to see this."

So much for dinner.

Pope rose and followed the twenty-something rookie to the tech office down the hall. The bank of televisions and computer monitors were dark until Tommy tapped his mouse. Three monitors lit up.

"So, I was running through our victim's desktop computer. It was clean. Not so much as a minute-long stop by a porn site. No lewd emails. No threats on the President's life. Or even our Mayor's." Tommy laughed.

Pope did not.

"Anyway, something felt wrong."

"Too clean," Pope offered.

"Exactly, everyone has something to hide. So, I checked his hardware. There was a disc in a portable driver. It was a kid's movie. Or, so I thought. At least that's how it was labeled." The tech specialist cued up the movie.

The lighting was poor, but Pope could make out a small structure made of painted concrete blocks. White porcelain sinks lined one wall. The camera panned swiftly across the hazy mirrors above the sinks and caught several bathroom stalls in the picture. The image came to rest on the first urinal in a line of four. A boy of about ten years of age, dressed in a T-shirt and shorts, was standing with his back to the camera. He was peeing with gusto. The boy's stream could be heard in the audio. The cameraman's breathing was heavy and slow.

"Go back to the mirrors," Pope said.

"Already cued up here, Detective." Tommy pointed to a second monitor.

The image was fuzzy, but Pope was sure it was Addison Ellis.

"Are there more of these?" Pope asked.

"I've viewed 23. Kids on a playground, playing soccer, and more bathroom scenes. But, I think there are more." The tech specialist pointed to the stacks of DVDs on the cart beside his desk.

Pope remembered the tower of movies in Ellis's house.

"Anything more . . . disturbing?" Pope asked.

"More of the same. Voyeur shit." Tommy shook his head.

"Can we tell where they're shot?"

"They're all shot at a park."

"There's a park just a few blocks away from Ellis's house," Pope recalled. "Can you print me off some stills, so I can compare them to the park? And, we'll need them to identify the kids, as well," Pope sighed.

"I'll do it and drop them on your desk."

"Nice work. Thanks."

Pope left the office and returned to his desk. He grabbed his cellphone and checked the time. It was 5:17 p.m. in San Diego. Roane should be just finishing her piano practice.

Chapter 5

New York, New York

Erica stood beside Julian in an otherwise empty elevator. His left arm tightly clasped his research papers to his chest. His right hand was shoved into his pocket, where his fingers wrapped around a plastic Ziploc bag.

Julian kept his eyes on the buttons on the elevator control panel. They were heading to the seventh floor. He smiled inwardly. The first verse of the Old Testament, in the original Hebrew, has seven words. The oldest book in the New Testament, Mark, begins with seven words. A good omen? While iconography inaccurately celebrated five wounds, Jesus actually suffered seven wounds at crucifixion: flagellation, the crown of thorns, the wound in the side, a nail through each hand, and a nail in each heel. *So, is seven a good or bad omen now?*

"So, the John Porter cipher led you to the tarot deck?" Erica watched Julian in the reflection of the elevator doors.

"Yes. Once I deciphered the value of the code, it pointed to Cosway's deck. Finding the deck was the hard part."

"Why do you argue the cipher's solution isn't John Porter?"

Julian found the corresponding sheet of the grimoire and held it against the elevator wall. He pointed to the alpha-numeric code in the center of the page.

"The cipher reads, *nh4z retr4p*. The accepted solution is that, by ascribing the letter *o* for the 4 and the letter *j* for *z*, the solution is *nhoj retrop*. So, it is a backward cipher for John Porter.

"But," Julian continued, "if that were the case, wouldn't the words be reversed as well? And why do they ascribe the letter *o* to the number 4? Sure, the *o* is the fourth vowel of the English alphabet, but if you are using a substitution cipher, then why wouldn't the seemingly non-ciphered *e* become the number 2 or 5? And, why does *z* become *j*?" Julian shook his head slowly, replaced the page into his stack, and removed his tie.

"But John Porter works in context of the remaining text," Erica argued. "And, there are numerous simple ciphers sprinkled throughout the grimoire."

"True, but another researcher made notes in the margins near the Porter cipher and attributed the text to John Weston, not John Porter. Why? What did that researcher uncover?" Julian countered.

They had reached the seventh floor. The elevator doors opened, and Julian followed Erica out of the carriage.

"So, what's your solution to the cipher?" Erica pointed down the hall to their right.

They walked side by side.

"Using the English alphabet, I used a true substitution cipher. The letters became numbers and vice versa. That gives you 148, *D*, and 26. In numerology, 148 could be treated as 1408. Using the Bible as source material, 1408 is the numeric value of the word *savior*. Likewise, in Gematria, 26 is the numeric value of the word *God*. The number of generations between King David and Christ is 26, as well."

Erica nodded and raised her brow. "But, what about . . ."

"The letter *D*? It created a challenge," Julian interrupted. "Looking at the cipher, the numbers stand out. I took that to mean they required a different key. I used the Hebrew alphabet. The letter *D* can be ascribed to the fourth letter in Hebrew. It's called the *dalet*. The dalet is used to represent God in Judaism."

The duo stopped before the door labeled 715. Julian thought of Paul's confession in his letter to the Romans: "For I do not understand my own actions. For I do not do what I want, but I do the very thing I hate."

"So, within the first part of the cipher you discovered three codes for the name of God," Erica confirmed as she used her key card to unlock the door. "What did your key reveal in the second part?"

"Nothing."

"Nothing? You said you solved the cipher." She pushed the door inward.

"I lied."

Julian shoved the curator to the floor and kicked the door closed behind them. He quickly withdrew a small, blunt revolver from his jacket pocket and pointed it at Erica.

"You scream, you die."

Chapter 6

Denver, Colorado

"Hi, Daddy."

"Hey, Sweetheart. How was piano practice?" Detective Pope asked his daughter as he sat in a nearly empty squad room watching the light snow fall outside.

"Okay. But I'd rather learn the trumpet."

Roane's voice was angelic. Pope was happy there was still an innocence in his daughter that had remained even after the divorce. He flipped the screen shots from Addison Ellis's home movies over on the desk. He wanted to hold his daughter tightly and never let go.

"Are you still at Mrs. Kennedy's?"

"Yup. Out front on her porch. Marcus is practicing inside, and he's horrible. It's better out here."

"Sweetie, you shouldn't be outside by yourself. Not even on Mrs. Kennedy's porch. Go back inside."

"But then I have to listen to Marcus. And, I can't hear Mom when she pulls up."

"Your mother can come to the door. Go back inside." Pope hoped she missed the tension in his voice.

"Mom's here now."

Pope heard his daughter's feet slapping the sidewalk. He pictured her backpack, which was nearly as tall as she was, flapping against her back as she ran. He could hear the pleasantries exchanged between mother and daughter, followed by an overtly loud, smacking kiss.

"Honey, I love you." Pope spoke more loudly to pull his daughter's attention back to the phone.

"I love you, too, Daddy."

"Before you hang up, can I speak to Mommy?"

Pope heard his daughter pass him off.

"Hello, Oren."

"I don't want her waiting for you on the street," Pope insisted.

"She wasn't on the street. She was on Mrs. Kennedy's porch."

"Either way, Sara, she should be waiting inside. Not outside on her own."

"Oren, she's perfectly safe on the porch. Mrs. Kennedy lives in a great neighborhood. You're being paranoid."

"Mrs. Kennedy's focused on her next appointment. She has no idea what's happening on her porch."

"I'm not doing this, Oren. You can't parent from a thousand miles away."

"It's not my fault you took our daughter to San Diego."

"Isn't it?"

"I . . . You didn't need to go so far . . ." Pope's voice trailed off.

"Oren, Roane is perfectly safe."

Pope cleared his throat. The tightness remained.

Sara added, "She's happy. And she's getting very good at the piano."

"She wants to play the trumpet!" He abruptly ended the call and dropped his phone onto the desk.

Pope could see his face reflected in the computer monitor. His eyes were wide and wild. He had shown much improvement in his anger management in recent months, but this Ellis case and its disturbing videos brought out the worst in him. And, there was just something about his ex-wife's voice that irritated an old wound.

Chapter 7

New York, New York

Julian quickly surveyed the room. Two queen beds, a bath, a small desk, a small couch, and a spectacular view of Central Park and the skyline beyond the window. In the corner of the room, near the desk, was a metal attaché case.

Erica Lyall sat motionless on the floor with her legs tucked under her.

"I want you to sit on the loveseat. Don't do anything stupid. You could still survive this. Understand?"

With tear-filled, wide eyes, the curator nodded her understanding.

"Good." Julian waved the gun toward the back of the room. "Go sit on the loveseat."

Erica was shaken. As she stood, her body twitched as if she were a marionette. She stumbled to the small couch.

Julian pointed the revolver at his captive with his right hand. His left hand dug into his jacket pocket and retrieved a small, spiral-bound notebook. He tossed it to Erica. From the desk, he retrieved the cheap ballpoint pen and uncapped it. He stepped to his prisoner and handed her the pen.

"Write down your full name and birthdate."

"What?" Her mind was uncomprehending, and her voice was weak.

"Full name and birthdate. Now!"

Erica found a clean sheet in the notebook and scratched her name and date of birth in a shaky, looping hand.

Julian snatched the notebook from the curator. He pointed the gun at the center of Erica's breast as he did some calculations. *The numbers would not lie. The tongue could lie, but the numbers were truth.* He nodded once he had the solution, and lowered his arm.

"I'm sorry for this, but I had to be sure," he said as he retreated to the desk.

"Who *are* you? Sure of what?" Erica's voice rattled.

"I'm who I said I am." He lifted the attaché case off of the floor and placed it on the desk top. "I had to be sure you are you." He put the gun back into his pocket.

Erica stared at Julian, then glanced to the door across the room.

"You could have just asked for ID!" she spit out.

"That can be faked. Don't run for the door. I'll shoot you in the back before you touch the latch."

Erica swallowed audibly.

"What do you want?"

"I told you. I need to examine the grimoire pages you purchased."

"That's why I was bringing you up here!"

"What comes out of the mouth defiles a person," Julian explained.

"Huh?" Erica shook her head.

"Matthew 15. Paraphrased."

"What are you, some kind of religious nut job?" Erica's voice was now steady.

Julian shrugged. "Maybe." He peered over his shoulder at her. "Let's not find out."

The steel in his eyes sent a chill through Erica.

"I believe the answer to the cipher is in these pages."

"So, you *did* solve the cipher."

Julian nodded. "I did. Substituting the number 4 with the fourth letter of the Hebrew alphabet, called the dalet, was the key."

"You said . . ."

Julian's glance stole the words from Erica's mouth.

"I had to change the cipher key once more. Dalet is represented by the pictogram of an open door in Hebrew. I understood it to equate to the solution. Otherwise, it was a simple number substitution cipher. So, *nh4z* equates to 14 plus 8 equals 26. Or, 22 equals 26."

Julian pulled the grimoire pages from the attaché case and laid them on the bed. Each was in nearly pristine condition. He began to put them in sequential order, using the blue page numbers in the corner of each sheet.

"There are 22 letters in the Hebrew alphabet and 22 trump cards in a tarot deck."

"I don't understand."

"The first part of the cipher is the key to the second part. The 22 trump cards equate to the 26 letters of the English alphabet. I spent five years rummaging through antiquarian shops in London. Then, four months ago, I found Cosway's tarot deck."

"So, Cosway gave you a tarot reading from the grave?"

Julian shook his head as he leaned over the bed and examined several of the pages. The handwriting was not the same as that in the Folger's portion of the book of magic. He knew, because he had become very familiar with all the idiosyncrasies of the known portion of the book.

Julian believed the handwriting on the pages strewn on the bed was that of Richard Cosway.

He responded, "I first believed that to be the case, but you can't have a duplicate card appear in a tarot reading. And, I learned from my research that Cosway didn't practice tarot. The second part of the cipher, *retr4p*, is not about what the cards *mean* but what they *hide*. Cosway was an artist, a miniaturist who used the artwork on the cards to conceal a message."

"Seriously, you found a hidden message on the cards?"

Julian nodded. He pulled a Ziploc bag from his jacket pocket. Inside the bag was a pack of tarot cards. He tossed the bag to Erica. She failed to catch the bag, and it fell into her lap. Tiny fragments of the cards littered the bottom of the bag.

"Jesus! You need to be careful with these!" she cried out.

Julian's eyes flicked to Erica. "Don't use the Lord's name in vain!" he hissed between bared teeth.

Erica's face went slack with fear. "I'm sorry." She lifted the bag. "It's just that these are rare, and fragile."

"They're trivial, but the power of His name is not." Julian turned back to the pages on the bed.

Erica looked toward the door once more. It was the only exit in the room, and Julian blocked it. She could try to run, but she knew her chances were slim. She shook her head and then turned her attention back to the large, intricately decorated cards. *What the hell, she was always a sucker for a good puzzle.* That's probably what drew her to Shakespeare in the first place. She thought of Shakespeare's mysterious Mr. W. H. and his beguiling, dark lady.

Erica gazed at the tarot deck through the plastic. Creases, tears, foxing, and flecking were visible on many of the cards. She unzipped the bag, carefully pulled the stack from the plastic, and placed it on the low coffee table in front of her.

"What was the solution to the second half of the cipher?" she asked.

"I was left with *retr4p*. I did another substitution. *R* became 18, the number of the Moon card. *T* became 20, the Judgment card. And so on."

Erica found the Moon and Judgment cards in the deck. Each of the trump cards was marked with a Roman numeral.

Julian continued, "But the letter *e* and the number 4 stood out. I knew that the cursory answer to the cipher was *John Porter*, so why was one vowel treated differently than the other? I guessed the *e* meant the card to be viewed upside down. As if it had been dealt in reverse. And, I guessed the 4 meant I should look at the back of the card. I guessed correctly on both counts."

Erica pulled the Pope card, the Emperor card, and the Tower card from the deck, as well.

"Your cipher requires you to use the Moon card twice?"

"Correct. Right side up and upside down." Julian picked up one of the pages and held it up to the light of the window. He put it back on the bed.

Erica studied the Moon card carefully. It was beautifully drawn and painted. A dog and a wolf howled up to the profiled face of the moon, while a crayfish crawled out of the lake below. The edge of the moon image looked somewhat smudged. She squinted and brought the card closer.

"Here," Julian said.

Erica looked up to see him offering a magnifying glass.

"Thanks," said Erica, taking the glass and holding it to the card.

Letters appeared on the edge of the moon.

She squinted. "It says *forward*."

"Yes. And, at the bottom of the card, written upside down, is the word *down*," Julian responded.

Erica found the second word written across the crayfish's tail, at the bottom of the card.

"I'll save you some time. The answer to the cipher is, *forward, reverse, up, down, left, right*."

"What the hell does that mean?" she asked.

"Death," Julian responded flatly.

Chapter 8

Denver, Colorado

Pope was still seething after his conversation with his ex-wife. And, it didn't help that he had spent the last thirty minutes looking through the still photos the tech specialist had pulled from Ellis's movies.

With the help of Google Maps, he was pretty sure he had identified the park near the victim's house as the scene for all of the videos. Pope would have uniforms patrol the park in an effort to identify the restrooms, soccer fields, and playgrounds for total accuracy tomorrow, but it seemed like the obvious choice. Identifying the children in the videos would be much more difficult.

With the snow now falling steadily and the forecast growing to fourteen inches, Pope decided to head home; otherwise, he would spend the night at the precinct. The 13 inches of day-old snow already on the ground would make the ride challenging as it was. Tonight's storm would bring the week's total to nearly three feet.

Pope bundled up and made his way to the parking garage. He got in his utility vehicle, started it, and silently praised the City of Denver for making a wise choice when selecting its new fleet of vehicles. The ride home in a sedan would have been extremely difficult. He turned left out of the garage and pushed through a short wall of snow.

The streets were empty. Pope actually enjoyed the calm and silence a snowstorm brought to the city. Flashing lights a few blocks to the west attracted his attention, as did three snow plows moving in formation near Coors Field. A dark figure stood shaking a fist in their wake.

Pope circled the block, came back to the scene, and quickly assessed the situation.

Someone had been digging out a car from an embankment of snow, and the passing plows had erased that person's efforts in one passing.

Pope stopped his vehicle, flipped on his service lights, and stepped out onto the white streets.

"Excuse me, can I help you?"

The figure holding the shovel was dressed in a hooded cape, like Little Red Riding Hood. The fabric wasn't red, though, but dark blue, nearly black.

The figure turned and lowered the hood. It was a woman, her white-blond hair tucked atop her head in a neat bun. Perspiration smoothed the stray wisps against her porcelain skin. Her cheeks and nose were red from the cold.

"Thank you, Officer. But, I'm afraid this mountain is more than either of us can move before those demons return!" She shook her shovel after the plows.

"Can you get a ride from someone?" Pope asked as he looked up and down the street. "You're not in an emergency route, so you can leave your vehicle overnight. We'll mark it with safety cones."

The lady leaned against her shovel and shook her head. "I know of no one with a vehicle capable of reaching my destination."

"I can take you home," Pope offered.

"Really? That is very kind of you, Sir."

"Hand me your shovel."

She did as instructed and stretched her arm out to offer the shovel. Pope grabbed it and then dug a narrow path to her. She raised her hood once more and then took Pope's hand. He helped her to the nearly cleared pavement in front of his vehicle.

"Thank you," she said, her voice betraying relief at being rescued.

Pope led her to the passenger door. Her skirts and cape billowed as she climbed into the seat. Brown buttoned boots stuck out of white ruffles. Pope opened the rear door and threw the shovel onto the floorboards. From the utility area, he then withdrew two orange safety cones. He stepped back to the pile of snow and placed them at the boundaries of the snow-covered vehicle.

Pope's brow furrowed as he rounded his vehicle and climbed back into the warm cabin. His passenger's appearance was strange.

"Where to?" He flipped off his emergency lights.

"Bannock and 13th, if you please."

Pope rounded the block and headed south.

"I'm Detective Oren Pope," he said after several long moments of silence.

"It is a pleasure to meet you, Detective. I am Ursula Deshayes. And I am so glad you happened by as you did."

"No problem. Glad to help."

The entire passenger side of the cabin was nearly filled with Ursula's dress.

"Are you an actress or something?"

"An actress? My heavens, no."

Pope expected more, but his passenger was not forthcoming. He found Broadway to be clear, so he turned right.

"Do you work near the ballpark?"

"I own a shop very near the snow pile we just left behind." Ursula slipped a finger under the tall collar of her dress.

"Sorry, are you too warm?" Pope turned the heat down.

"Thank you."

"What kind of shop is it?"

"I own the Harvest Moon," she replied.

"Is that a restaurant?"

"It is a book store, among other things."

"Mrs. Deshayes . . ."

"Miss," she interrupted.

Pope smiled. "Ms. Deshayes, are you trying to be illusive?"

"Only as much as you are trying to be coy." She smiled and unbuttoned her cape.

"What?" asked Pope, now perplexed and intrigued.

"Direct questions result in direct answers."

Pope shook his head. "Fine. What's with the getup?"

"I happen to like clothing of a bygone era. Women dressed with such elegance just before the turn of the twentieth century. I emulate that style. The short of it is, Detective, I like it."

"Was that so difficult?"

"Difficult? No, not at all. Only, it is a response that I am forced to duplicate with every new introduction. I chose, on this occasion, to have some fun with it."

Pope shrugged. "You must want the attention. I mean, your fashion stands out."

"No, I simply wear what I like to wear."

"Okay, I get it. How about your book shop?"

Pope turned onto East 13th Avenue.

"The Harvest Moon is an occult shop."

"Occult? You mean, like tarot cards, and crystal balls, and potions, and stuff? Is there much money to be made?"

"My home is just on the right."

Pope's gaze followed her gesture. Beside a towering high-rise apartment building, he saw a large wooded lot bordered by a gray stone wall. Beyond the wall, in the center and crest of the lot, a large, red-brick Victorian mansion in pristine condition towered.

"I do okay." Ursula winked.

Pope made a low whistle. "I guess you do." He put the vehicle in park and turned on his emergency lights once more. "I'll make a path to your door."

Ursula nodded.

Pope shoveled a narrow canyon up the short cobble stairs to the slate walkway. By the time he reached the mansion's front porch, he had worked up a sweat and shed his hat and gloves. He turned to see Ursula making her way between the walls of snow.

"Would you like to come in for some refreshment, Detective?"

"Thank you, but no. However, I just had a thought. There's a case I'm working on that may touch in your area of expertise."

"Is that so?" Intrigued, Ursula raised an eyebrow.

"Would you be willing to help?"

"It would be the least I could do to repay your chivalry."

"Great. Thanks. I'll stop by your shop sometime tomorrow evening, if that's okay."

"I will await your call." Ursula handed a business card to Pope. "And, thank you again for your assistance."

"Glad I happened along." Pope turned and retraced his path to the street.

"Indeed," Ursula whispered.

Chapter 9

New York, New York

"Death? That's the solution?" Erica asked with a sense of foreboding.

Julian nodded. "Death. I realized I was missing something. There is a space between the two lines of the cipher. So the empty space becomes a character in the cipher. An unmarked, unnamed space. The thirteenth trump card is commonly known as the Death card. But, it's actually untitled. Unmarked. Unnamed."

Erica breathed deeply at the revelation. She found the thirteenth card and examined it. A skeletal man stood over several dead bodies, which seemed to be underwater or buried shallowly. The image reminded her of costumes worn in the *Dia de los Muertos* celebration she had seen in Mexico. Erica used the magnifying glass to study the intricacies of the artwork. At the top of the card, just before the Roman numeral *XIII*, she saw the letter *P*.

"There's a *P*."

"Yes," Julian flatly responded.

"So, what does it mean?"

"Page 13." Julian snatched a grimoire page from the bed with a flourish. "Page 13."

Despite the circumstances, Erica was intrigued. She rose from the small couch and stood beside Julian as he read the antique script.

The page looked much like the other pages in book of magic. The ink was iron gall, except for a blue numeral, written by a more modern hand, at the top of each page. The script was written on off-white pulp paper. Small, hand-drawn flourishes denoted the start of a new charm or incantation. There were many inscribed symbols on the page, as well. Erica recognized them as those of an alchemical table developed in the fifteenth century. A familiar word square dominated the bottom third of the page.

"This can't be it," Julian protested.

The paper shook in his hands.

"What were you expecting to find?" Erica took a step back.

"His name!" he barked.

"Cosway?"

"What? No, not Cosway! The name of the curse on our world!"

Erica took another step back. "You're looking for a *curse*?"

"Shut up!" Julian crumpled the 200-year-old paper in his trembling left hand. "Let me think."

He scrubbed his right eye with his palm. "Page 13. Page 13. It must be on page 13. That's the answer. The solution to the cipher. The cipher . . ." he muttered as he paced the room.

Erica retreated into the corner of the room, beside the small couch. She warily watched Julian as if he were a big cat in a cage. She needed to get out of the room before the cage door opened. She inhaled for a calming breath and took stock of the tarot cards on the table.

"Palindrome," she said.

Julian's head snapped up. "What?"

"The words on the tarot cards. *Forward, reverse, up, down, left, right*. Essentially, they are the definition of a palindrome, a word or phrase that reads the same backward or forward. And, there's a palindrome on that page." Erica pointed to the manuscript sheet crumpled in Julian's hand.

"What?!"

Erica took a tentative step toward the distraught Julian.

"The word square. It's a palindrome."

"Yes, but . . ." Julian uncurled the grimoire page and smoothed it against his chest. "It's the Sator Square. This version is not unique. There's nothing special about this square."

"Not special? Not unique? It's the most famous word square of all." Erica extended a hand and slipped the page from Julian's grip.

"Of course, but it's not unique to *my* research. It must be in hundreds of surviving copies of grimoires. In fact, it's on a page in your own book of magic," Julian countered.

Erica nodded. "I know. Page 146." She examined the word square. "But this version is not encircled by the names of the Magi, like the one on page 146."

"Still, it's exactly like dozens of other examples around the world." Julian shook his head. "It can't be the solution."

Erica read the text on the rippled page above the Sator Square. It was a list of Latin words. That came as no surprise; although the text was mostly in English, Latin had been used on multiple occasions throughout the grimoire. But, something about what Julian had just said and these words tickled Erica's imagination.

"Does this list of names mean anything to you?" she asked.

"They are just names!" Exasperated, Julian stepped closer and snatched the sheet from Erica's grip.

"Please be gentle with that!" she protested.

"Sorry." Julian's demeanor changed once again.

"Just above the square, there's a list of names in Latin."

"So?"

"These are place names. Locations around France and one in Britain."

"I don't recognize them." Julian looked to Erica with sad, pleading eyes. "Can you help me?"

"If I help you, will you let me go?"

"Of course." Julian reached into his pocket, pulled out the gun, and handed it to Erica. "I never meant to hurt you anyway."

Erica, astonished at how quickly the tables had turned, stared at the gun in her hand. It was surprisingly heavy.

She gazed into Julian's troubled eyes. "If you try to hurt me, I'll shoot," she promised.

He forlornly shook his head. "I won't hurt you."

She nodded. "OK, then. Albenate and Leucae are the Roman names for Aubenas and Loches in France. Corinium is the modern-day city of Cirencester in England."

Julian pulled a small, leather-wrapped journal from his inside jacket pocket. He quickly scratched down each city name.

Then he paused, looked up, and suddenly smiled. "Aubenas?"

"Yes, does that mean something to you?"

"It aligns with my research. She mentioned Aubenas in her letter."

"Who did? What letter?"

Julian reached into his jacket and withdrew yet another plastic bag. An envelope was enclosed. He handed it to Erica.

Julian chuckled. "It's been right in front of my face. Hiding in plain sight."

He replaced his journal into his jacket, quickly turned, collected his tie from the floor, and walked out of the hotel room.

Erica stood in wide-eyed stillness. In one hand she held a plastic bag with a letter and in the other hand she held a revolver. The grimoire pages were still spread out on the bed, and a deck of tarot cards worth thousands of dollars was on the table.

"What the fuck?" she asked the empty room.

Erica carefully laid down the gun and bag with the letter, taking equal care with both. Then she went to the desk and snatched up her cellphone. She dialed 9-1-1 and then collapsed onto the small couch. Her eyes traveled to the table. She could see the envelope through the plastic bag. It was addressed in a beautiful script that spoke of a time when handwriting was an art form.

"9-1-1, what's your emergency?" the voice in her ear asked.

But now the envelope riveted all her attention. She picked up the plastic bag and blinked several times at the paper within.

"9-1-1, are you on the line?"

Erica read the address aloud. "Monticello, Virginia."

"Ma'am, you're speaking to the 9-1-1 call center in Manhattan, New York. Are you in Virginia?"

Erica shook her head in disbelief and began to laugh.

"He had a letter addressed to Thomas Fucking Jefferson?!"

Chapter 10

Denver, Colorado

The store was poorly lit. Two skylights overhead normally would have supplied some light, but they were covered in snow. There was a strange odor in the air. Bookshelves lined each wall and stood like sentinels on each side of the narrow aisle that led farther into the store.

The shelves subsided, and the store opened up slightly. Tables were littered with candles, stone vessels, and statues of all sizes. Intricate charms and talismans lined the display case that also served as a sales counter.

Behind the counter sat a young woman dressed completely in black. She was reading a paperback with rolled pages and a tattered cover. The dark eye that wasn't covered by jagged bangs flitted from the book. It assessed Pope as he approached. She hitched a thumb over her shoulder towards a doorway behind her and then dove back into the book.

Pope stepped around the counter and followed the short hallway to the partially opened door. He knocked softly before entering.

Ursula Deshayes sat at her desk. Her posture was perfect. Her platinum blond hair was perfectly coiffed. Her dress billowed out around the wooden-slated desk chair. She looked more like Mary Poppins than an occultist.

"Good afternoon, Ms. Deshayes."

Ursula spun in her chair and removed a tiny pair of metal-framed glasses.

"Hello, Detective."

"I passed the pile of snow that is your car. Looks to be in once piece. Glad to see you made it in today."

"Thank you. The city did a fine job of clearing the streets overnight. Moina, the young lady at the desk, was kind enough to shuttle me in today."

"Your tax dollars at work." Pope nodded. "Would you mind taking a look at something for me?" Pope tapped a manila file folder against his palm.

"That is why you are here, is it not?"

Pope smiled. He crossed the small office and placed the folder on Ursula's desk. She replaced her spectacles and pulled several photos from the folder. She studied each carefully.

Pope spoke. "I think that's an athame, correct?"

"You are correct, Detective. Athames are used in the Wiccan culture. They are ceremonial blades that represent one of the four elementals in Wiccan tradition."

"This one happens to be a murder weapon."

Ursula gasped.

"It was found in the chest of the man pictured in the other photo."

Ursula flipped to the driver's license photo of Addison Ellis.

"Ever see him before?"

"I do not believe so." Ursula shook her head.

"Would you mind checking your records to see if he's ever been a customer?"

"I would not mind at all, once you produce a warrant." Ursula looked up from the photo.

"A warrant? Really?" Pope smiled.

"Of course, Detective. My customers are, shall we say, on the fringes of society. If they were to find out that I was sharing their information with the authorities, then my business would suffer."

They stared at one another for a long moment.

"I will file for a warrant right away. I wouldn't want to put your business, or that big house of yours, at risk," the detective said snidely.

"Thank you."

"Back to the knife. Do you recognize it?"

Ursula arranged the four photos of the athame on her desk, placing them side by side. She ran her hand over two detailed images of the blade and two of the handle.

"Size and shape are what I would expect to see of mass-produced versions of an athame. The intricate scroll work on the blade is unusual, though. And the inlays in the handle are unique."

"Do you sell many athames?"

"No."

"Any patrons with a knife fetish?"

"Not that I am aware of."

"Are you familiar with the symbols on the athame's handle?"

Ursula studied the photos again. The first inlay she examined was a chevron pointing in the direction of the blade. A pointed, thin, straight line bisected the chevron. The second design was that of a floating circle above a crescent shape. It looked like a ball dropping into a bowl, or a one-eyed smiley face.

Ursula removed her glasses and turned to Detective Pope.

"I would not expect to find either of these symbols on an athame," she began. "The carpenter's square and the spear," she tapped the bisected chevron, "are Roman Catholic symbols."

"Roman Catholic, are you sure?" Pope queried.

Ursula smiled. "You are surprised someone in my business would know of such symbols?"

Pope shrugged.

"I was raised Roman Catholic, Detective. I know chapter and verse very well. It is surprising you do not, considering your surname."

"Very funny. I'm actually quite familiar with the Bible, thank you." Pope cracked a smile. "It's the other crap I don't know. Please, enlighten me."

"The square and spear are iconographic symbols for Saint Thomas. He was attributed with building the first Christian churches in India, hence the carpenter's square. And, he was martyred with a spear."

"Odd thing to put on a knife," said Pope.

"Agreed."

"And the second symbol?" he asked.

"Well, if we treat this item as simply a knife and not an athame, then the second symbol seems less out of place. It represents the Greek mythical character of Charon. Are you familiar with him?"

"Aside from their military might, I am not familiar with the Ancient Greeks," Pope confessed.

Ursula raised an eyebrow. "Were you in the service, Detective?"

Pope nodded. "Two tours in Afghanistan."

"You may have heard Charon referred to as the ferryman. He was charged with carrying souls to the underworld across the river Styx."

"Okay, yeah. I've heard that before. That seems an accurate symbol for a murder weapon."

Ursula agreed.

"I initially thought the builder's square to be a chevron. Like patches on a uniform," said Pope. "Could this symbol be used for something like that?"

"Your knowledge of military history will be superior to my own," responded Ursula. "But, it seems possible. Could it be the insignia for a certain battle or a platoon, perhaps?" Ursula asked.

"That's what I'm thinking. I'll run with that and see if something pops."

Ursula smiled up at Pope.

"You've been a great help. Thank you, Ms. Deshayes."

"Glad I could return the favor. Should I expect you back with your warrant?"

"You were serious about the warrant?"

She nodded.

"Then, I guess I'll be back in a day or two."

"I will look forward to your return."

Ursula rose and shook Pope's hand. He gave her a smile and then made his way past the sales counter.

Moina never batted an eye.

Chapter 11

Denver, Colorado

The three men huddled closely on the pews of St. Paul's and spoke in whispers. The afternoon light filtered through the images of the apostles in Tiffany stained glass. The large, vaulted ceiling of the nave carried their words farther than they liked, but the offices were already occupied by the church board members who were attending their monthly meeting.

"You should have asked!" Charles's tone was biting.

"I know. I'm sorry." Julian handed the envelope containing $13,000 over the pew.

Charles snatched the envelope.

"The important thing is that you found it." Dominic smiled. "What do we need to do?"

"I'm not sure yet. I must do more research," Julian responded. "But, we're close. Any luck with your recruitment?"

"Two synagogues and the basilica are willing to listen," Dominic responded.

"Makes sense. Jews and Catholics are more superstitious than the

Protestants." Julian opened his journal and found the latest entry. "We must contact the priest of the Church of St. Laurent in Aubenas, France."

"I can do that," Dominic volunteered.

"Good. I'll research Loches and Cirencester." Julian added, "Charles, I need you to lean on the Protestant churches. We need to have as many on board as possible."

Charles nodded. "Addison Ellis's body has been found."

Julian's face went slack. His eyes fell to his lap. He rubbed his chest.

After a moment of silence, Julian met the other men's gaze. "We're lucky it took as long as it did. Bateleur was clever. He must have known of the auction. He nearly foiled our plans."

All three men nodded.

Julian handed his journal to Dominic. "Hold onto this. Keep it safe. If anything happens to me, then follow the instructions I wrote on the back cover."

"Nothing's going to happen to you," Dominic reassured.

Julian shook his head. "Bateleur is targeting me. It's just a matter of time."

Movement at the front of the church caught their attention. The sexton came through the door to the bell tower. He was severely stooped, and he shuffled like a penguin. He stopped when he caught sight of the three men in the pews. "I'm sorry. I thought the church was empty." His bushy, white mustache bounced as he spoke.

"It's okay, David. We were just finishing up," Charles called out.

The sexton moved closer. His smile grew when the short distance compensated for his nearsightedness.

"Two pastors and a priest sitting in the nave, with me up front. Something is terribly wrong with this picture. Don't stand too close, the lightning bolt may take you with me." He chortled.

"David, you're as righteous as any of us," Father Dominic replied.

"And, I'm no longer a pastor." Julian stood.

"Nonsense. Once a pastor, always a pastor." David shook a finger. "You were one of the greatest men who ever led this church. No offense, Pastor Charles."

"None taken."

"Pastor Julian was the heart and soul of this church," the sexton added.

Pastor Charles smacked the heavy envelope against his palm. "Well, I should get this back to where it belongs. Let's talk tomorrow."

The three men dissolved their meeting and left David to clean up the nave.

Chapter 12

Denver, Colorado

Pope poured himself another cup of terrible coffee from the fickle coffeemaker that sometimes brewed a pot but just as often hissed, sputtered, and left the grounds dry. He sipped on the bitter brew as he crossed the offices of the Major Crimes Division. He pinched the bridge of his nose. His eyes ached. He had begun looking at the photos of children from Ellis's movies just before dawn. Now the sun was up, and the office was bustling with civilian support staff clocking in for the day.

"Good morning, Partner." Max Prebys filed in behind Pope and clapped a hand on his shoulder. "Can you believe this snow?"

Coffee sloshed over the rim of the mug and down Pope's hand.

"Morning." Pope shook away the spill.

"You're at it early," Prebys said.

"Couldn't sleep." They had reached their desks near the middle of the room. Pope sat his mug on the desk. "I've been looking through the stills from Ellis's movies. I might have found something."

Pope handed Prebys one of the photos. "On this kid's backpack. Is that a Blessed Sacrament patch?"

"The school?" Prebys squinted at the picture of a young boy standing near a swing set. "Could be. Yeah, I think it is. Nice work."

"At least it will narrow our search."

"Then, what? If we get lucky, one of these kids recognizes Ellis. But, the odds of the kid shedding light on who killed Ellis are miniscule."

"I'm liking a parent of one of these kids as our guy. Or, maybe it's one of these boys all grown up and back for revenge." Pope rubbed his chin. He had forgotten to shave.

Prebys nodded. "Good theory. But, we've got a tough road ahead."

Pope agreed.

"Hey, you attended St. Paul's downtown, right?" asked Prebys.

"Yeah, when I was a kid." Pope raised his eyebrows at his partner. "Why?"

"My boy was over for dinner last night before he went on duty. He said a warrant was issued for the pastor there."

"Really? I've not met the new pastor."

"No, this guy used to be the pastor there."

"Pastor Julian?"

"Yeah."

"What's the warrant for?" asked Pope.

"It's out of New York. Apparently, he attacked a woman there. He had a gun and forced his way into her hotel room."

"Pastor *Julian*?" asked Pope in disbelief. "I don't believe it."

"Isn't he the guy who lost his family in that school shooting years ago?" asked Prebys.

Pope nodded.

"Well, maybe he finally crossed the line between broken and unbroken."

"Maybe," said Pope, who knew that blurred line, as well.

Chapter 13

Denver, Colorado

Father Dominic D'Angelo practiced his sermon from the lectern at St. Paul's. His flock would be expecting his best on Saturday evening, and he did not intend to disappoint. His sermon series on the mysteries of the parables had captivated the crowd; the final installment this Saturday would bring down the house.

Father D'Angelo was happy to have been placed at St. Paul's. It was a unique church. It shepherded both the Lutheran congregations on Sunday and his own Catholic congregation the evening before. This allowed the churches to better serve their communities. And, they did so seamlessly. St. Paul's benefited from a mixed denominational board that wanted to see the church as a whole flourish. Outside of the services themselves, all other functions were jointly sponsored. Picnics, fundraisers, and community outreach were joint ventures. It was both unique and beautiful.

The narthex door opened. A child was silhouetted by the morning sun. Father Dominic marked his sermon notes and then stepped down from the lectern to meet his young visitor. The child had already started down the aisle.

"Good morning, may I help you?"

"Father, I'm in need." The young girl's voice was tiny in the big space.

Interesting choice of words for a child.

She was slender, but well-dressed in a heavy coat and clean jeans. Her blonde hair shone like moonlight. She wasn't one of the street children who visited the church on Mondays for a meal, but she looked familiar.

"What can I do for you?" Father Dominic sat down on a pew so they could make eye contact.

"I was told to come to you." Her eyes were on the floor.

She kept her hands buried in her coat pockets. Her shoulders thrusted forward.

"I'm here to help you," Father Dominic prompted.

Her eyes flicked up for just an instant.

"You can tell me anything you like." Father Dominic smiled. "Let's start with your name."

Her eyes held his for nearly ten seconds.

"Maddison," she responded in a whisper.

"It's nice to meet you, Maddison. I'm Father Dominic." He added in a whisper, "But, you can call me, Dom."

Maddison's mouth twitched into a half smile.

"Sometimes, my friends call me Dommy." He chuckled. "Sounds like *dummy*, huh?"

The little girl smiled, but she kept her distance and left a space on the pew between them.

"I know. It's silly," said the priest, attempting to win the child's confidence.

"He was right," Maddison said.

"Who was?"

"Jesus."

"Jesus?"

"Yeah, he said you were nice."

"Jesus said I was nice? Jesus talks to you?"

She nodded. "Sure. We're friends. Doesn't he talk to you?"

Dominic's smile faltered. "I like to think so. I think he talks to me in my prayers. Is that what you mean?"

She shook her head.

"Then how does Jesus talk to you?"

"With his voice, Silly."

"You hear his voice in your head?"

"No, I hear it, with my ears. We talk, just like you and me." Maddison touched her small lips.

"Do you see Jesus?"

"Sure." She nodded.

"Well," Father Dominic hesitated, "You are very lucky."

"I know." She lifted her chin. "He told me so."

Dominic was certain he had seen this young girl before. "Why did Jesus send you to talk to me?"

"I'm supposed to help you."

"I can always use some help. Am I supposed to help you, too?"

She shook her head. "I help you, then I help myself. After that, I can see my Mommy again."

Maddison pulled a small gun from her pocket and pointed it at Father Dominic. It was the size of a toy, but Dominic knew this wasn't a game.

"Maddison, what's that for? This is very dangerous. Someone could get hurt." Dominic struggled to keep his voice steady.

"It won't hurt long. Then God will take away your pain." Her angelic smile sat in contradiction to the vile gun in her hand.

"I think you might have misunderstood Jesus. I don't think Jesus wants you to shoot me."

"He does, I know he does. He just told me to. He brought me here, and he gave me the gun." Maddison looked proud.

Dominic considered leaping from the pew, but she held the gun steady and with confidence. His mind raced. *Could one reason with a child of nine or 10?*

"Maddison, tell me about your Mommy," he implored.

"She's in heaven. I miss her."

The gun shifted slightly. Dominic forced a smile.

"I'm sure you do. My Mommy's there, too. I miss her. Sometimes, I get real sad. But, I know that she's up there looking down on us. So, I try to make her proud of me. I do the best I can, so that she'll be happy watching me. You know what I mean?"

"Yup. I was sad until Jesus spoke to me. He said Mommy was sitting with God, and that she would never stop loving me."

"That's very true. Whether your Mommy's here or with God, she will always love you. And, she wants you to be happy."

"I want to be happy."

The gun waivered.

"I can help you be happy. Let me help you." Dominic stretched a hand out toward the fragile girl.

"You will." Maddison pulled the trigger three times.

The blasts caught Dominic by surprise. It was intensely loud. He winced at the thrumming in his ears. Then, a fire started on his right side, just under his armpit. His breath was wet and thick, viscous like honey, but not sweet. It tasted of copper or iron. The pain grew. It radiated. He looked down and saw his black clerical shirt darkened across his stomach, and his pants darkened at his thigh. From the narthex he heard a man cry out.

Dominic turned to see Julian enter the nave. The movement caused severe pain, and he canted in the pew. He could no longer see his attacker. He tried to mutter a prayer, but his voice gurgled in his chest. He listened to Julian's footfalls.

They stopped short.

Dominic heard his friend gasp.

"Hello, Daddy," the small voice called out.

"Caroline?" Julian's voice was tight.

Dominic understood why the little girl looked familiar. She looked like a picture he had seen of Julian's child. But she had been killed in a school shooting seven years ago. Did this child just look like her? Or was it really she, returned from the dead?

"Caroline?"

Dominic heard the tears in his friend's voice.

"Jesus has a message for you, too, Daddy." Her voice was still clear and soft. "'Bateleur says, goodbye.'"

Then, another loud concussion rang through the church.

Chapter 14

Denver, Colorado

Ursula Deshayes removed her glasses and rubbed her eyes. Something about the athame wouldn't let her rest; the use of a Christian symbol on a Wiccan knife was intriguing. She was convinced that the builder's square and spear must have different meanings in this case and had combed the internet for more than an hour in an attempt to find the symbols used elsewhere.

There were a few candidates within the U.S. Army shoulder sleeve insignias, but they were not identical. Spear tips, arrows, and missiles were pictured on several patches, but none paired with a builder's square or chevron. The Army's Cyber Command used three spears in its insignia, but the chevron was missing. Maritime insignias used the carpenter's square but with a plumb bob or a fire axe and maul.

Ursula replaced her glasses. She moved the warrant for her sales records aside and set the two photos Detective Pope had given her side by side on her desk. One pictured the right side of the athame's handle, the other showed the left. On the right side was the bisected chevron that she believed to be the carpenter's square and spear. On the left was the floating circle above the crescent, which was the symbol of Charon, the ferryman of the underworld. A symbol of Greek mythology and one of Christian mythology, seemingly disconnected.

The carpenter's square was judged as an instrument used to create perfection in ancient civilizations, including the Greeks. A Greek was said to have invented the tool in the sixth century, and it was of great importance to the mathematician Euclid, the father of geometry. So, it was impossible for the carpenter's square to represent a single object or person in Greek mythology.

Ursula turned her attention back to the Charon symbol. Was it possible that the symbol wasn't Greek, after all? Could it be Christian?

Joseph, Jesus's worldly father, was often represented in medieval art with a carpenter's square. This was based on a belief that he was, in fact, a carpenter. The original Greek translation used the term *tektón* as Joseph's trade, which meant he was a craftsman or artisan, and so it was an easy step to carpenter. Was the pointed line dividing the square another building tool?

If they were Christian symbols, then two saints were represented on the athame? Saint Joseph on one side and Saint Thomas on the other.

Ursula recalled her college studies of the stained-glass windows of gothic churches in Europe. She remembered a saint being depicted in a boat on a river near a castle. She stood and retrieved a large, frayed-edge book from the shelf above her desk. *The Golden Legend* was the second bestselling book in medieval Europe, surpassed only by the Bible. A collection of hagiographies by Jacobus de Voragine, *The Golden Legend* was printed sometime in the thirteen century. To an art student like Ursula, it *was* the Bible.

She cracked the mid-twentieth-century printing of *The Golden Legend* and flipped through dozens of pages recounting the lives and deaths of Catholic saints. Nothing jumped out.

Ursula typed a web search into her laptop. Nothing of interest returned. She then typed, "Catholic saint ferryman." She was rewarded for her effort.

She picked up her antique phone and dialed Detective Pope's number. The detective answered after three rings.

"Detective, I found something regarding those symbols," she said enthusiastically.

"What did you find, Ms. Deshayes?"

"Both symbols could be construed as Christian. Charon was the Greek ferryman, but there was also a Catholic ferryman. Saint Julian the Hospitaller. He fought in the crusades and was . . ."

"Did you say *Julian*?" Pope interrupted.

"Yes." Ursula was taken aback at the detective's rudeness. "So, you have Saint Julian on one side of the knife and Saint Thomas on the other. Does that mean something to you?"

"It does. Julian Thomas was just escorted into my precinct."

Chapter 15

Denver, Colorado

Pope watched the interview from beyond the two-way glass. The man sitting at the table across from fellow detectives Wallis and Trainer looked unkempt, thin, and dissociative. Pope wouldn't have recognized him if they had met on the street. He looked nothing like Pope remembered as a teenager. Pastor Julian had then been boisterous and vibrant. The man at the table was weathered and dull.

Detective Wallis finished reading the material and closed the file. He looked across at the prisoner.

"Do you understand why you've been arrested?" he asked.

There was no response. The man rocked slowly and scratched at his chest.

"Mr. Thomas, can you hear me?"

Still no reply.

"Were you recently in New York?" the detective persisted.

The pastor's brow knitted. He stopped rocking. He whispered, "Page 13. I had to see page 13."

"That's right." Wallis nodded. "Do you remember Ms. Erica Lyall?"

Julian rubbed his chest.

"Do you remember assaulting Ms. Lyall?"

The former pastor did not respond.

"What happened today, Mr. Thomas?" Detective Trainer leaned onto the table. "Did you see what happened?"

On the other side of the glass, Pope winced as he watched Julian rock back and forth with his head down. He looked like a man on the edge of sanity.

Wallis and Trainer continued to ask similar questions of their prisoner, but Julian was nonresponsive. He just rocked and rubbed his chest. The detectives looked toward the glass and nodded toward the door.

Pope and Prebys met them in the hallway.

"I think that guy's lost it," Wallis suggested.

"It doesn't look good," Prebys shook his head.

"May I talk to him?" Pope asked.

"You think he might be involved in your case?" Trainer asked.

"Maybe. Maybe not. But, I do know him, and I'm sure he'll remember me. Maybe I can get through to him."

Trainer and Wallis exchanged a glance.

"Can't hurt. But, I don't think the man you knew is in that room," Wallis clasped Pope on the shoulder as he and his partner exchanged places with Pope and Prebys.

Pope and Prebys stepped into the interview room. Julian never lifted his eyes from the table. His rocking had slowed. Prebys took a position in the corner of the room, while Pope took a seat across the table from the distraught pastor.

"Julian, it's been a long time," Pope said.

There was no response.

"Do you remember me?" the detective persisted.

The pastor's eye flitted to Pope for a brief instant, but he did not reply.

"PJ, it's Oren Pope. I went to your church as a boy. You know my parents."

Julian's brow knitted. He stopped rocking. He whispered, "Maeve and Ewan."

"That's right." Pope smiled. "PJ, do you know where you are?"

"Of course. I'm in jail." His voice was steady.

"And, do you know why you're here?"

"Murder." His head was bent. His eyes never left the table.

"You're currently being held for assaulting Ms. Lyall in New York." Pope leaned across the table. "But, tell me about the murder."

The pastor's eyes remained on the table. He rubbed at his chest.

"Who was murdered?" Pope prodded.

"Father Dominic, Ellis, Cody Siler, Katie Dunst, Bobby Liddell, Tony Santana, Denise . . ." Julian rocked more violently, "and Caroline. . . no, not Caroline! . . . I saw her! She was there today."

Pope was shocked. First his childhood pastor assaulted a woman in New York. Then he's found at the church where a kid shot the priest. And now PJ mentions Addison Ellis among a list of murder victims.

From the corner, Detective Prebys asked, "Is that a confession?"

Pope scowled at his partner. Then he wrote down the list of names Julian had spoken. He circled Cody Siler and marked it with a question mark. He stood and pushed the tablet to the viewing glass so the detectives on the other side could read it.

"You mentioned Ellis. Who's Ellis, PJ?"

"He goes by many names," the pastor responded.

"Did you kill him?"

"'Whoever strikes a man so that he dies shall be put to death.'"

Pope recognized the verse from Exodus. He and Prebys exchanged a glance.

"PJ, a body has been positively identified as Addison Ellis."

The pastor's eyes darted up to hold Pope's gaze. "But, could you positively identify his soul?"

"His soul? What do you mean?"

His former pastor's eyes sank back to the table. "It's something we all should consider. Is your soul safe?"

"You're right, I should go to church more often," Pope retook his seat.

"'With thankfulness in your hearts.'"

"PJ?"

The pastor's mouth twitched. "I asked if your soul was safe, not your spirit. I spent my life raising people's spirits to the Lord. Have you read Hillman?"

Pope shook his head. "I don't know him."

"I met him once." Julian smiled. "It was a brilliant lecture."

"You've lost me PJ." Pope tapped the table with his pen.

"There's another dimension to each of us. It's intrinsically part of you. I never truly understood Hillman's distinction between the spirit and the soul. Even after I met him. That is, until now. Or rather, until this quest began."

"You're on a quest?" Prebys asked from the corner.

Pastor Julian sat tall and swiveled his head. The look in his eye caused

Prebys to straighten.

"My quest is complete." He turned back to Pope. "Yours is just beginning."

"Was your quest to kill Addison Ellis?"

The pastor shook his head. "It was to save his soul."

"By killing him?"

"No. He was already dead. 'And the dead were judged by what was written in the books, according to what they had done.'"

Prebys nodded to Pope. He made a pushing motion with both hands. He wanted his partner to press the subject. He could sense the confession was at hand.

"It was too late. I couldn't save him."

"PJ, did you murder Addison Ellis?"

"I couldn't save him." Pastor Julian began to sob. His rocking and scratching started anew.

A knock came to the door.

"PJ, we're going to get you some coffee." Pope stood. "We'll be right back."

There was no response.

Prebys followed Pope out of the room.

In the hall, Wallis and Trainer waited with a printout from a case file dated October 13, 2013. Pope took the sheet and read through it quickly.

"Do you remember this case?" Wallis handed the sheet to Prebys.

"School shooting." Prebys nodded. "Yeah, I remember. Fourteen-year-old kid named Cody Siler went to school with a gun and started shooting. He killed three kids plus himself that day."

"Why did your friend say he did it?" Detective Wallis asked.

Pope ignored the question. "The scene today at the church, the girl killed the priest, right?"

"Looks that way. The priest is barely alive, in surgery right now," Trainer said. "Then she killed herself."

Pope nodded. "PJ . . ."

"What's with calling this guy PJ?" Prebys interrupted.

"That's what we called him as kids. PJ, for Pastor Julian," Pope clarified. "He also named his wife and daughter in that list. They were killed in a school shooting, too." Pope continued, "His daughter was ten at the time, and his wife was the principal of her school. A kid walked in with a gun and killed eight people that day."

Pope stared at his partner. "So, this is not a confession. He's taking credit for crimes we know he didn't commit."

"You're right. Sorry," apologized Prebys.

"The guy's lost it. He said he saw his dead daughter today," Trainer said.

"The photo I saw of the little girl who did the shooting looked a lot like Julian's daughter." Pope rubbed his chin. "I think we have enough to keep Julian here for a few more days. Ellis's murder trumps New York's assault charges."

"Yeah, but without any hard evidence, the NYPD is going to get our boy," Prebys added.

The detectives agreed.

"Are you guys okay with me pursuing the questioning?" Pope asked Trainer and Wallis.

"I think you're wasting your time, but sure," Trainer responded. Wallis nodded his approval.

Pope clasped Prebys's shoulder. "Let's see what else we can pull out of him, Partner."

"I'll grab the coffee."

Chapter 16

Denver, Colorado

Ursula used her laptop to search sales records for purchases by Julian Thomas. He had been a repeat customer over the past five years. Julian had asked Moina make several special orders from other occult shops around the world for him. But, he had never purchased an athame from her. His interests seemed to lay in grimoires and medieval manuscripts only.

Ursula made a hard copy of the records and also saved the files to a thumb drive. She made a copy of the warrant then slipped the original, the copy of the sales records, and the thumb drive into a large manila envelope for Detective Pope. She stepped out of her office and approached Moina.

"Moina, you wrote some requisitions for several grimoires for a man named Julian Thomas. Do you remember him?" Ursula asked her lone employee.

Moina looked up from her tattered, dog-eared book.

"Yeah. He had a thing for old books. Keen on Gematria and the Kabalah, too."

"What was he like?"

"Old. Kind of odd, but nice enough. He didn't talk much, which I loved. He'd hand me a request. I'd write up the requisition. He'd pay. He'd leave. Spent a lot of money."

"Do you know if he was interested in the subject matter, or was he simply a bibliophile?" Ursula leaned her hip against the display case. Her corset pinched a little.

"Subject matter," Moina nodded. "He didn't care about condition, as long as he could read the pages."

"Did he ever mention Wicca? Or Greek mythology?"

"Wicca? Greek myths? Nope." Moina pushed her bangs from her eye. "Why all the questions?"

"I think he's in some trouble."

"Like, with the law? I heard you talking to your police detective."

"Yes, I believe he is."

"You know, that cop's pretty cute. For an old guy."

"Detective Pope is not old."

"I meant like your age."

Ursula shook her head and turned back toward her office.

She asked over her shoulder, "Did Mr. Thomas mention what he was searching for?"

"Bateleur."

"The Magician? Did he say why?"

"Nope. But, he was only interested in the French representation of Le Bateleur."

Chapter 17

Denver, Colorado

"Mr. Thomas, I got some coffee for you." Prebys set the cup down, and then took the seat across from their prisoner. "I'll apologize in advance for the quality, but I thought you could use it."

Pope laid a palm full of sugar packets and creamer cups onto the table, then took a position near the door. He and his partner had agreed to reverse roles.

Julian ignored the cream and sugar. He cradled the hot brew between his hands and sipped.

"Pastor, let's back up. How'd you know Addison Ellis?" Prebys asked.

Julian rested the cup on the table's edge. "I've been tracking him for twelve years."

"Tracking him?"

"Since my daughter died."

"You think that Ellis killed your daughter?" Prebys prodded.

Pope stiffened.

"Brandon McKay killed my daughter. And, my wife. And, six other children that day."

Pope relaxed a bit. It seemed there was still some of the man he once knew in there, after all.

"What's Ellis have to do with McKay?" Prebys asked.

Julian grimaced. His hand jerked to his chest, spilling the coffee. He began rocking again and rhythmically muttered something barely audible.

Pope stepped closer. He listened intently. He withdrew a notebook and quickly made a few notes.

"Rev. Thomas? Pastor, are you okay?" Prebys asked.

Julian kept rocking and muttering.

Prebys looked to Pope.

"PJ, tell me about your daughter," Pope said.

The rocking slowed.

"Tell me about Caroline."

Julian became still. He placed the nearly empty cup back on the table.

"She was eleven, right?"

Julian shook his head. "She had turned ten in April. She didn't want a party. She wanted to work in our church's soup kitchen instead. We were so proud of her. She invited all her friends to join her. Caroline was perfect."

"I remember her. She was seven—no, eight—years younger than me. She was so sweet. You and Mrs. Thomas raised her right."

"We were proud of her."

"PJ, you were saying something under your breath a minute ago. Do you remember what it was?"

Julian looked to Pope. His real confusion was obvious. He shook his head.

"PJ, we're going to get something to clean that up." Pope pointed to the spill. "We'll get you some more coffee. And something for you to eat. We'll be right back."

Prebys was startled but quickly rose and followed Pope out of the room.

"Did you hear what he was saying?" Pope asked after the door closed.

"He was just muttering. A prayer, maybe?"

"He was reciting the Quran."

"The Quran? What's a Christian pastor doing reciting the Quran?" Prebys asked.

"Julian has multiple doctorates in religious studies. I'm sure at some point he studied the Quran."

"How do *you* know the Quran?"

"I was stationed in Kabul. I studied it, too. To better understand the people who surrounded me," Pope responded.

"What did the pastor say in there?"

"He mentioned genies."

Chapter 18

Denver, Colorado

Ursula placed several volumes from her library onto her desk. Each was opened to pages devoted to Le Bateleur. Most discussed his position as the first trump card in the tarot deck. Some discussed his change in appearance, from one artist's rendering to the next. In the popular Waite-Smith deck, he was simply titled The Magician, but looked more like a Greek philosopher in a long, white robe. In the Tarot of Marseilles deck in which Julian Thomas was interested, Le Bateleur was depicted as a street performer wearing a wide-brimmed, rakishly tilted hat and playing games of chance on a small table surrounded by a crowd.

This same rogue was also pictured in Collin de Plancy's *Dictionaire Infernal*, printed in France in 1899. Julian Thomas purchased it from Ursula's shop two years ago. Students of the occult coveted this book on demonology, which was in continuous publication for nearly a century. The 1899 version was illustrated by Louis Le Breton. In it, Le Breton depicted 69 different demons in terrifying detail; this was interesting, because the artist was better known for his naval and maritime paintings.

"Ursula, I checked the shelves. There was this manuscript page that Julian Thomas never picked up." Moina handed the plastic-sheathed page to her boss.

Ursula replaced the *Dictionaire Infernal* on the shelf to make room on her desk for the discolored page.

It was made from pulp paper and in terrible condition. The script was written in Arabic by an artistic hand. A translation of the page was included. Ursula realized that she was looking at pages from a century-old copy of the Quran. It was, specifically, the last *sirha*, or chapter, of that holy book.

> *I seek refuge in the Lord of mankind,*
>
> *From the evil of sneaking whisperer,*
>
> *Who whispers into the hearts of men,*
>
> *From among the Jinn and mankind.*

"I guess Mr. Thomas was into Islam," Moina said. "I don't remember him ordering anything else like this."

"I reviewed his order history. He was on a search, but I cannot divine for what he desired."

"Any idea what a Jinn is?" Moina asked.

"In Islamic tradition, the Jinn are one of the three of Allah's creations. Angels and humans round out the triumvirate. In Europe, the Jinn later became known as genies."

"Genies? Like from the lamp?"

"You are correct in referencing *Arabian Nights*. But, to Muslims, the Jinn are not just folklore. They exist with us and, like humans, are either good or evil. They whisper in our ears and manipulate us to do their bidding."

"Creepy weird," said Moina.

Ursula pondered the statement.

"In this case," she responded, "perhaps more than we yet realize."

Chapter 19

Denver, Colorado

Detectives Prebys and Pope reentered the interview room. They were carrying another cup of coffee and a stale cheese Danish from the vending machine, along with a roll of paper towels.

Julian was sitting calmly and twirling a sugar packet on the table near the spill.

Pope placed the fresh cup of coffee and pastry onto the table. Prebys pulled several towels from the roll and began to mop up the spilled coffee.

"Can you hand me that wastebasket?" Prebys asked.

Pope grabbed his partner's arm, staying him from wiping away the mess.

"Do you see that?"

Near the spill were several lines drawn with sugar.

"Is that a Jewish star?"

"You mean the Star of David." Pope leaned over the table.

Prebys shook his head. "Your pastor quotes the Bible, he quotes the Quran, and he draws Jewish symbols?"

"Not exactly. I mean, yes, and no. I don't think it's a star. Do you see those dots inside and outside the lines?"

Pope looked to his childhood pastor.

Julian just continued to spin the empty white packet.

"PJ, why'd you draw this?"

The pastor did not respond.

Pope used his phone to take a picture of the shape drawn in sugar on the table. Then he seated himself across the table and faced Julian.

"We brought you some more coffee. And, a Danish. PJ, are you hungry?"

"'In hunger, and in thirst, and in nakedness, and in want of all things,'" Julian said. His voice was a whisper.

"Was that Deuteronomy, Pastor?" Pope queried. Prebys stared at his partner in disbelief, but Pope didn't break his gaze on Julian.

Julian nodded.

"From the Bible, or the Torah?"

The pastor's eyes met Pope's gaze.

"D'varim," he responded.

"The Torah, then. You're a learned man, PJ. What's this symbol?" Pope pointed to the lines of sugar.

The pastor followed Pope's finger. His eyes widened, as if seeing the shape for the first time.

"That's the Seal of Solomon!" Julian dropped the empty paper packet. "I drew that?"

"You don't remember drawing this?" Prebys asked.

Julian shivered and rubbed at his chest.

"PJ, what's the Seal of Solomon?"

"It's a talisman against evil."

"You need to be protected?" Pope asked.

"We all need protection!" Julian responded and then began to rock.

"'The Lord is faithful. He will establish you and guard you against the evil one,'" Pope quoted a verse from Thessalonians.

Prebys gave Pope a look of amazement. Pope shrugged.

"You're quoting the Bible to *me*?" Julian huffed.

"Sorry, PJ. But, I had a good teacher."

Julian's face softened. A smile took root. He stopped rocking.

Pope smiled.

"PJ, can you explain how you knew Addison Ellis?"

"I can try. But, you must keep an open mind."

Pope nodded.

"I wanted to make sense of what happened."

"With Mr. Ellis?"

"No, with Caroline and Denise. School shootings have become an epidemic, and our state seems to be at the epicenter. I wanted to know why. So, I studied the facts of the cases. Not just Caroline's, but from around the state, and around the country. I found similarities. Good kids would snap because of bullying or hazing."

"There's more to it than that," Prebys spoke up.

"Yes, there is. How well do you know the cases?" Julian asked.

"I've not studied them," Pope admitted.

"I was interested in the murder-suicide cases. Like Caroline's. The surviving shooters could express themselves. The dead could not. I used my influence as a pastor to gain access to families, friends, first responders, and the detectives. I worked the cases, to borrow the phrase, while continuing to care for my congregation. But, I became obsessive, and then I couldn't manage both. I knew that I had to make a choice. Initially I chose my congregation. But then I decided to take one last look. That's when I found something."

Pope and Prebys leaned in expectantly.

"Each of the shooters was carrying $1.06." Julian smiled.

The detectives exchanged a glance.

"Of course, you don't understand." Julian shook his head. "Sorry, my mind seems foggy." He shook his head and then explained.

"Each shooter was carrying exactly one dollar bill, one nickel, and one penny. Exactly."

"Okay," said Pope, "so what?"

"Don't you find that odd?" Julian asked.

"Sure," Pope agreed. "But, it could be a simple coincidence."

"Maybe, but each one of those nickels was a buffalo nickel," Julian said with a grin.

Pope looked to Prebys and cocked his head.

"Thousands were minted, but I bet you could scour this building and not find a single one stuffed in anyone's pocket. But, the *age* of the nickel was the true sign that something darker was transpiring."

"Wait, each kid had a buffalo nickel that was minted in the *same year*?" Prebys asked.

"Minted in the same year, minted right here in Denver, and all had the rare, three-legged buffalo image. Something to do with a flaw in the die at the mint." Julian nodded.

"The odds would be staggering," Pope agreed. "But, what does it mean?"

"I asked myself that for years, and then five years ago I solved it. I combined the amount with the year the nickel was minted. $1.06 and 1937. Psalms 106:37."

"Help me, PJ. I'm not familiar with that verse," Pope pleaded.

Julian trembled and rubbed his head.

"You okay?" Pope asked.

"Could I have that?" Julian pointed to the Danish.

"It's yours."

Julian took a bite of the pastry and chased it with a sip of the coffee. He chewed slowly and stared at the brew.

"Better?" Prebys asked.

"I can't remember the last time I ate."

The edges of Pope's mouth pulled down in sympathy for his pastor.

"You were telling us about the Psalm," Prebys coached.

"Psalm 106, verse 37." Julian cleared his throat. "'They sacrificed their sons and daughters unto demons.'"

Chapter 20

Denver, Colorado

Ursula sat at her desk in her tiny office surrounded by books, photos, and copies of receipts. Her notes in a small tablet were creating an interesting inventory of purchases Julian Thomas had made from her shop.

Her cellphone chirped.

Ursula studied the screen through her small, round spectacles. It was a text message from Detective Pope, with a photo attached. The message simply stated that Julian Thomas had drawn the symbol in the photo.

Ursula looked at the image and inhaled in surprise when she saw the Seal of Solomon.

Then she laid down her phone and again picked up Julian Thomas's inventory list.

Of course. The former pastor's pursuit was now becoming clear to her: Julian Thomas was looking for a talisman against evil. He must have believed that he or someone he knew was being manipulated by a jinni, demon, or some other evil spirit and that the Seal of Solomon could control those demons.

Ursula rubbed her temples in an effort to recall her knowledge of the Seal of Solomon.

According to legend, the seal was on a signet ring that angels gave to King Solomon. It was made of brass and iron and inscribed with "the Most Great Name of God." Solomon used the power of the ring to enslave a number of demons to build his colossal temple in Jerusalem.

Islamic tradition added four varying gemstones to the face of the ring; each was believed to be a gift from a different angel. Julian represented the gemstones in his sugar drawing with four dots at the compass points surrounding the six-pointed star.

Ursula did not believe the ring ever existed. But, could it be that this pastor *did* believe in it? And that he was searching for it now? And if so, what or who were the demons he needed to control?

She gathered her cellphone and returned a text to Detective Pope.

Chapter 21

Denver, Colorado

Pope's cellphone rang. He glanced at the screen and saw a returned text from Ursula Deshayes. He opened the message and furrowed his brow. He read, "Be careful. You are dealing with dark elements that are difficult to understand."

Pope stuck the phone into his pocket.

"PJ, I'll admit what you found is intriguing and disturbing, but what's it have to do with Addison Ellis?"

"I involved myself in the Siler case in Fort Collins. I ingratiated myself with the detective handling the case, and I counseled the Siler family. That's how I learned that Cody had a pen pal. His mother thought it was part of a school program."

"Do they still do that in school?" Prebys asked.

"I checked with the school. They do not."

"Did you find the letters?" Pope wrote a note to follow up with the school.

"No. But, the family allowed me to go into Cody's bedroom, where I found an envelope in his dresser drawer. It was one of those small, manila pockets. Tiny, but large enough to hold a nickel."

"The forensic team missed it?"

Julian shrugged. "I made the detective aware of it. He had it finger-printed. Along with Cody's print, there was a partial that could not be identified."

"That's some good police work, PJ." Pope smiled and made a note to contact the Fort Collins detective.

"I was always a fan of cop shows on TV."

"You said the print was unidentified. Is this leading to Ellis?" Prebys asked.

Julian nodded. "I checked into the other school shooting cases. In four other cases, the parents of the shooter knew their child had a pen pal. But, no other evidence showed up. Too many prints on the money to make a conclusive connection. Then, one day, Addison Ellis walked into my church."

"Your church?"

"Sorry, I still think of it as mine. Ellis walked in and spoke with Pastor Charles at St. Paul's. He told Charles he had information concerning Caroline's case. Ellis asked Charles to pass along his contact information to me. He left his address. So, I tailed Ellis for a week."

"Why didn't you call the police?" Pope asked.

"He was filming kids in the park, in the bathroom. I had to confront him." Julian closed his eyes and began to rock.

"Pastor, if the creep was involved in my child's death, I would have killed him, too," Prebys confessed.

Pope shot his partner a look.

"PJ, maybe you didn't intend to kill him. Maybe the confrontation got out of hand. Maybe it was self-defense?"

Julian continued to rock. He held a hand to his head as the other rubbed at his chest.

"PJ . . ."

The persistent knock at the door interrupted Pope's question. Prebys opened the door. A remarkably tall man ducked under the doorway to enter. He was dressed in a cheap, olive-green suit and carried a worn, leather briefcase.

"Detectives, I was hired by St. Paul's Lutheran and Catholic Community Church to represent Rev. Thomas."

Peter Rota handed Prebys his business card.

"My client will answer no more questions at this time. I am concerned with his health and wish to have him remanded to a hospital for a doctor's examination."

The lawyer sat his briefcase onto the table and examined a file from within.

"Detectives, I understand that a warrant has been issued for my client's home. It's not in this paperwork. I'll need to see it immediately."

"Rev. Thomas has not requested counsel, so he is free to continue this interview without your interference, Mr. Rota." Pope stood.

"My client is not of sound mind and as such is unable to request counsel, Detective."

Pope watched PJ rocking. It was true that his former pastor did not look well. Pope feared the pastor's anguish had finally broken him. Pope was sure they had enough to keep Julian in Denver, so maybe it was best to tend to the man's health before pushing him further.

Pope nodded his approval to the lawyer. "I'll bring you the warrant."

Prebys followed Pope from the interview room. They walked back to their desks. Pope sat down heavily into his chair and rubbed his eyes.

"That guy's had a tough time of it," Prebys offered. "I would have snapped a long time ago."

"I'm worried about him," Pope agreed as he shuffled through the paperwork on his desk.

"If the story about the envelope and fingerprint is true, then maybe this case isn't so clear-cut." Prebys added, "He might have a chance with a sympathetic jury."

"I think the lawyer's planning an insanity plea." Pope stood. "Call that detective in Fort Collins. Ask him about Julian's story. I'll take this to the Jolly Green Giant." He waved the warrant.

As Pope rounded the corner, the interview room door burst open.

"I need help in here," PJ's lawyer screamed.

Pope ran down the hall and bursted into the room. The pastor was convulsing on the floor behind the table. He was prone, rigid, and shaking violently. Pope pulled out his cell, gave the dispatcher his badge number, relayed his location, and made his demands. He slid the table and chairs away from PJ and crouched beside him.

"What happened?" he asked the lawyer.

"He never said a word. He just grabbed his head and then fell off his chair."

"PJ, help's on the way. Hang in there," Pope implored.

Chapter 22

Denver, Colorado

"Now, before we go in. You can't touch anything. CSU is going to come in after we're done, but I wanted you to see everything in situ. Understand?"

Pope and Ursula stood outside Julian Thomas's house. A team of six CSU investigators stood on the front lawn in clean, white coveralls waiting for the detective to finish with the house. Pope stood with his latex-gloved hand on the door knob. In her nineteenth-century attire, Ursula looked strange tugging on her own blue latex gloves.

"I understand, Detective. I only hope that I can be of assistance."

"I hope so, too." Pope twisted the knob and stepped into Julian's house.

The living space looked much like Ursula expected from a widowed, suburban former pastor. A Roman cross hung on the wall adjacent to the front door. Pictures of his wife and daughter were placed prominently throughout the house. A shallow layer of dust covered most surfaces, and a table tray sat opened near a recliner facing the television.

"Back here," Pope called over his shoulder. "What I want you to see is back here."

Ursula followed the detective down the short hallway to a dark room. Pope stepped into the room, and after an audible click the room was bathed in a harsh, incandescent light.

"I had to drag this lamp into the room. The bulb had been removed from the overhead ceiling fixture," Pope explained.

Ursula saw dozens of candles around the room. Wax was caked around stumps of varying sizes. Around the room were well-worn volumes of manuscripts and books from medieval and contemporary times.

She assumed the room was at one time the master bedroom. A large bed had been disassembled and stacked in the corner of the room. The mattress and box spring had been placed against the window, where they effectively blocked the natural light behind the drapes and blinds. But, it was the *vesica piscis* at the center of the room that drew Ursula's attention.

The two interlocking circles were each approximately four feet in diameter, and they were set within a large rectangle.

"Any idea what those are for?" Pope asked following Ursula's gaze to the floor.

She crouched awkwardly in her corseted dress and examined the shapes.

"These appear to be created in salt. Do you agree?"

"Salt?" Pope peered more closely at the symbols. "Not sure. If so, what's the relevance?"

"Salt is an essential natural element," Ursula responded. "It was valuable and holy in ancient times. It is a physiological necessity for good health. It is part of us. Therefore, it is significant in occult practices. It represents the earth element for the Wiccan. But, I have never seen it used in a summoning spell."

"A summoning spell?" asked Pope.

"Understanding Rev. Thomas's infatuation with classic grimoires and his fascination with demonology, that would be my understanding of what is laid out before us," Ursula answered. "Would you mind?" She raised her hand for assistance.

Pope helped her back to her feet.

"I'll have Forensics analyze the circles." Pope scratched a reminder in his tablet. "So you think this matches your working theory of what PJ was up to."

"PJ?" Ursula smoothed her dress.

"Short for Pastor Julian."

"That seems rather informal, Detective."

"Julian Thomas was my childhood pastor. I had trouble pronouncing Julian as a kid. He suggested PJ. It stuck. All the kids my age began calling him PJ."

"Well, then, this case must be extremely difficult. I am sorry." Ursula eyes softened. "How is he doing?"

"The doctors have no idea what's wrong with him. They've induced a coma."

"Medical science may not be the answer." Ursula continued to investigate the room. "Do you still attend church?"

"I haven't been back to St. Paul's, or any church, for that matter, since returning from Afghanistan."

"Too bad. Having faith in something greater than ourselves is invaluable to the human experience."

Ursula slowly circled the room, her gloved hands clasped behind her back.

"What do you have faith in?" Pope asked.

"I believe the universe is mysterious, and intentionally so. I believe life should be spent trying to understand those mysteries."

"That's very transcendental of you."

Ursula gave Pope a polite smile.

"We should not attempt to define everything we feel. We should not be so linear in our thought process. We influence the matter of existence with our thoughts, with our beliefs. We should be careful with that power."

"You've lost me."

"We should open this discussion once more at a later date," Ursula suggested.

"I'd like that, but you'd have to dumb it down a little for me."

"I doubt that very much."

Ursula stopped in front of Julian's evidence wall. PJ had taped his school shootings' research to the wall in his empty closet. She studied the photos, newspaper clippings, and police interviews carefully.

"How does this fit into the case?" Ursula indicated the wall.

"I can't share too much, but it seems to be what was driving PJ. Sorry, Rev. Thomas. Were you in Denver 12 years ago?"

Ursula shook her head.

"Rev. Thomas lost his daughter and wife, Denise, in a school shooting. Denise was the principal of the elementary school. An 11-year-old kid named Brandon McKay walked into the school and started shooting indiscriminately. Caroline Thomas and six other children were killed. Denise attempted to take the gun from Brandon and was killed. Brandon then committed suicide."

"That is more than one man should bear." Ursula shook her head. "So, he then assumed a quest to solve the rash of shootings plaguing our state?"

"It seems that way." Pope nodded.

"Very interesting."

"Does this change your theory? Which, by the way, I'm still waiting to hear."

Ursula smiled demurely. "I forgot that I am working with a professional detective. You will not let me avoid the topic, will you?"

"No, Ma'am."

"Could we discuss it outside?" Ursula spoke warily as she looked around the room.

"Of course."

Ursula followed the detective out of Julian's house and into the cold light of a gray winter's day.

"It's all yours," Pope called to the CSU investigators. "There's a white, granular substance on the bedroom floor. I need a chemical analysis of it ASAP. Thanks."

The white-clad team marched into the house in single file.

Pope led Ursula to his vehicle and out of the cold.

After the heater started to hum, he prompted, "So, about this theory."

Ursula removed her latex gloves. "Have you ever heard of the Jinn, Detective?"

"I have." Pope nodded slowly.

"Then, you are aware of their manipulative powers over human beings."

Pope began to anticipate Ursula's working theory, and he did not like where it was headed.

"I believe Rev. Thomas was looking for a Jinni. Specifically, the Jinni who was responsible for the school shootings he was investigating."

"You don't really believe demons, or rather Jinn, are walking among us, do you?" Pope was incredulous.

"We are not discussing what *I* believe, Detective. We are discussing what your childhood pastor believes."

The two stared at one another a long, silent moment.

Detective Pope remembered PJ quoting the Quran's last chapter. He shivered and turned up the vehicle's heater.

Chapter 23

Denver, Colorado

The bell above the door chimed. Moina Porter looked up from her book to the old pendulum clock on her right. It always took about two minutes before the customer made it through the towers of books and stepped to the counter behind which she sat.

The man who appeared was a surprise. Moina had seen all kinds of people come into the shop, but this man was unique. At nearly eight feet tall, he was a giant. He wore a green homburg hat and a heavy, wool overcoat.

"Looks like we could get some more snow," he said.

The weather? Really? There were basically three salutations Moina expected of her lone male customers. There were the sorry saps who were looking for a talisman to improve their love life. They took the direct approach after making sure the shop was empty. Then, there were the serious occultists who glared at her but whispered their request. It was usually for a potion or serum. Finally, there were the amateurs mostly satisfying a curiosity by entering the shop. These guys always opened with the weather.

But this guy seemed too unique and self-assured to be in that latter category.

"How can I help you?" Moina asked, with thick incredulities. She carefully marked her page and set the paperback onto the counter.

The giant eyed the book.

"I love Barker! That looks like *Imajica.*"

Moina was surprised a second time by this guy.

"*Imajica* is Barker's best work! Don't you think?" He laughed. "Of course, you do. Your copy is in shambles. How many times have you read it?"

Moina shrugged.

"The universe he creates in that book is amazing. So well-thought-out. Every detail illustrated. He has you believing magic is real." He removed his homburg and set it on the counter. "And that Pie'oh'pah character is so sexy."

Moina actually blushed. It had been years since something embarrassed her. She often fantasized about Clive Barker's character slipping into her bed at night.

"Can I help you with something?" Her voice cracked. She craned her neck to meet his eye. His height involuntarily pulled her off her stool.

He smiled easily. "I'm looking for an amulet. Atia's sign. Do you have one?"

"I think so," Moina said and then looked down into her display case.

"I need one made from gold. As pure as I can get."

He splayed his long fingers on the counter and bent over so that his head was just inches from her own.

He smelled of spruce. But, not like cologne or soap. There was an earthiness about him. It seemed to naturally emanate from him, as if he *were* a tree.

Moina shook her head. "I definitely don't have that. Don't get too many amulets in gold."

"That's a shame. I was told gold has more power, and I need all the help I can get."

Usually, Moina would next collect her copy of *Imajica*, take her stool, and start reading. The dejected customer would take the hint and turn away.

But she asked, "Help with what?" Her words surprised her.

"I'm creating a film. It's my first. I could use some good luck."

"I have some other lucky . . ."

His easy smile and shake of the head stopped her in mid-sentence. "You know most of those things are just trinkets. I need Atia's sign."

Moina found herself blushing once again.

"I'm creating my film for my school's terminal project. I'll be graduating from CFS this year!"

"I tried to get into Colorado Film School last year."

Moina couldn't believe she shared that. She hadn't told anyone about her rejection from film school. Not even Ursula. And, Ursula was probably her closest friend. Maybe, her *only* friend.

"Where'd you get your bachelor's?" he asked.

"Bachelor's? I just graduated high school a little over a year ago."

His eyes were wide with disbelief. His smile turned into a chuckle.

"You can't be that young. You look more mature than that." He pointed to her book. "A teenager couldn't possible grasp *Imajica* as well as you obviously have."

"I'm nearly twenty." Moina brushed the hair from her eye and smiled. "I read it for the first time when I was fifteen."

"Fifteen? Wow. I wish I was that mature at fifteen. CFS doesn't know what it's missing. Is your interest in acting, production, or writing?"

"Acting?" She guffawed. "Do I look like an actress?"

He nodded shyly.

Moina eyed him suspiciously. "You're serious, aren't you?"

He blushed and gathered his hat.

Moina smiled again. Smiling didn't come naturally anymore. It felt good.

"Can I take your name and number?" She asked. She collected a pen and slip of paper. "I'll do a search for your amulet and give you a call."

Chapter 24

Denver, Colorado

Detectives Prebys and Pope stepped through St. Paul's narthex into the nave and shook the light snow from their coats. Pope tentatively walked up the aisle of the church. It had been more than a decade since he had been in the building. It was a bit unsettling. He found the insecurities and awkwardness of his teenage years fluttering out of the dark towards the light. *No matter the distance in space or time, your younger self remains buried within.* Pope found himself unexpectedly thinking about what Ursula might say on the subject of skeletons in the closet.

"Detectives," a tall, large man called out as he approached from the front of the church.

His gray hair had receded, and a symmetrical, round bald spot had developed at the top of his head. A perfect crown of hair appeared to ring his head. He could have been an actor cast for the role of Friar Tuck in the next film adaptation of Robin Hood.

"Pastor Charles?" Pope asked.

The three men met in the center of the nave and made their introductions. The pastor stood at least six inches taller than both detectives.

"Detective, how are your parents?"

"My Dad's still recovering from his fall, but he'll be back on his feet shortly," Pope responded.

"Good. We've missed them here on Sundays."

"I'm sure they'll be back soon."

"Pastor, you know why we're here. I think Rev. Thomas could use your help," Prebys suggested.

"Have you been to see him?" Pastor Charles asked.

The detectives shook their heads.

"I was there this morning. The doctors induced a coma. There was swelling of the brain. They're attributing it to excessively low levels of sodium in his body," Pastor Charles explained.

"I didn't know that was possible," Prebys said.

"My apologies for the loss of Father Dominic. I heard the bad news this morning," Pope said.

Pastor Charles looked down at his feet.

"Did you know Maddison Willet, the Father's shooter?"

The big man shook his head slowly.

"Her resemblance to PJ's daughter was uncanny." Pope asked, "Did you know Caroline?"

"No. But, I've seen pictures of her." Pastor Charles continued to study his shoes.

"Pastor, we're here because PJ told us Addison Ellis visited you," Pope prompted.

"That's correct." Pastor Charles looked up. "It was maybe a month ago. He came into the church and asked for me. Donna showed him to my office. Once she left, Mr. Ellis said he had information he wanted me to pass on to Julian."

"Information regarding the school shooting?" Prebys asked.

"Yes."

"Caroline's shooting?"

"He wasn't specific, but that's what I assumed. Mr. Ellis said Julian would be very interested in what he had to say."

"And that was it? No further details on what he intended to tell PJ?" Pope questioned.

Prebys pulled a photo of Addison Ellis from inside his jacket and handed it to the pastor.

"Is this the man who visited you?"

Pastor Charles studied the photo for a long moment.

"Is this an old picture?" he asked.

"About one year. It's an employment photo," said Pope.

"It's hard to say," mused Pastor Charles. "Hair color is right. And, his facial features are similar to what I remember. But, I can't be sure. How tall is this man?"

"How tall?" asked Prebys, confused.

"The guy who introduced himself to me as Addison Ellis must've been nearly eight feet tall," said Pastor Charles. "He makes me look short," he chuckled.

Chapter 25

Denver, Colorado

"Bonjour, Monsieur. Je m'appelle Prêtre Canacs, de Eglise Saint Laurent." The voice said over the phone.

"Saint Laurent? In Aubenas?" Pastor Charles asked.

"Oui. I am returning a call to Father Dominic."

"You speak English?"

"Oui. Of course," Father Canacs replied.

"Excellent. My name is Pastor Charles." He sat down heavily in his office chair. "Thank you for calling back."

"Father Dominic will be joining us on the call?"

"Unfortunately, no. He's . . . unavailable." Pastor Charles's voice cracked.

"Too bad. We had a spirited discussion regarding assisted suicide, and I had hoped to continue it."

"I'm sorry." Charles didn't know how else to respond.

"Oh, well," the priest resigned. "The Father was asking about our word square."

"Yes, what can you tell me about it?" Charles's pen was poised over his tablet.

"In our records, I found a letter written by the Abbot. It is dated 1149. I have just emailed it to you."

Pastor Charles dropped the pen and opened his email. A scanned copy of the Abbot's letter was attached. He opened the letter and strained to make out the looping script.

"This is in Latin."

"*Oui*. It was the language of the time. Vulgar, oui? But, our beautiful language was just being born," Canacs commented.

"Of course. I'm lucky. I'm rusty, but at least my Latin is better than my French."

"Rust, is lucky?"

"In this case, yes. Thank you, Prêtre Canacs."

"*Vous êtes les bienvenus*. Are you studying French folklore?" asked Canacs.

"I hope so, but I can't be sure."

"I do not understand."

"Good, and I hope you never have to. Thank you, again." Pastor Charles ended the call.

He magnified the medieval church record on his computer and began to translate the document.

Chapter 26

Denver, Colorado

"Peter Rota, Esquire, doesn't exist. *Never* existed, as far as I can tell. He certainly isn't registered with the bar in the state of Colorado. And, I can't find him registered in any other state. I think this guy's a ghost." Detective Prebys leaned against his desk.

"I have the stills taken from the security videos." Pope handed his partner the photos.

"Not too clear." Prebys squinted at the grainy image of the 7'10" Rota crossing the squad room on the day he posed as PJ's lawyer. "You'd think a police station would have better surveillance."

"Rota must have had a fake court ID. The duty officer obviously checked the guy in and got a signature." Pope pointed to a photo showing Rota talking to the officer behind the counter. "The last photo, the one with Rota at the elevators, is a little clearer."

Pope looked up, stood, and nodded toward the entrance.

A man of about sixty years of age crossed the room. He was short and dressed in a wool, three- piece suit. His graying hair was wiry and stuck out in every direction. With his neatly trimmed Van Dyke beard, the psychologist looked like a cross between Colonel Sanders and Albert Einstein.

"The doctor has arrived." Pope led his partner to meet their guest.

"Detective Pope, it is nice to see you again." Dr. Wesley Wernhart shook Pope's hand.

"Doctor, this is my partner, Max Prebys."

"Hi, Doc." Max took the doctor's hand. "You two know each other?"

The doctor nodded. "We've worked together in the past, yes."

Prebys looked to his partner. Pope shook his head almost imperceptibly.

The trio walked to the debriefing room and took their seats. The detectives sat across the table from their guest.

"So, you've had a chance to review the Thomas interview transcripts?" Pope prodded.

"Yes, I have. Rev. Thomas's behavior was erratic. The mumbling and dissociative replies to your questions cause me to believe the man had recently suffered a psychotic episode. And, from the notes you supplied regarding his current medical state, I believe his medical doctors will uncover a physiological cause. Possibly, a brain lesion or encephalitis."

"Would Rev. Thomas be capable of assault, or even murder, during this psychotic episode?" Prebys asked.

"Certainly. Psychosis results in personality changes, paranoia, difficulty with social interactions, and impairment of judgment. That includes the inability to determine right from wrong."

"What about this supernatural angle?" Prebys asked.

"Rev. Thomas is a spiritual man, so it seems plausible he would blame demonic elements for causes out of his control. Certainly he might direct his anger, or revenge, on a perceived evil," Dr. Wernhart responded. "I've written my diagnosis." He handed a folder to Detective Pope.

"Thanks, Doctor." Pope accepted the folder and shook hands with the man. "Can we reach out to you again if need be?"

"Of course." Dr. Wernhart shook Prebys' hand and exited the debriefing room.

"Is that your shrink?" Prebys asked.

Pope shot his partner a look.

"Come on, I knew you were seeing someone."

"Yeah," Pope huffed. "He was helping me out."

"That was when you cracked?"

Pope now glared at his partner.

"What?" Prebys held up his hands in mock surrender. "When I drew you as a partner, I had to do some checking."

"Maybe you should have asked me instead of listening to the rumor mill," retorted Pope.

"That's what I'm doing now, Partner." Prebys smiled. "It was that arson case, right?"

A shiver clawed through Pope.

"Guy setting people on fire?" Prebys clarified.

"Yeah. Stockton case. Three victims in two fires. Difficult case."

"But, you caught the guy."

"Yeah, he didn't make it too difficult. But, it was the . . . the burning . . ." Pope paused, then continued. "It reminded me of something I saw in Kabul."

"Hey, man. PTSD is legit. You're not the only cop, or war vet, I've known to be diagnosed."

"And here I thought I was special." Pope slapped his partner on the back and pushed him through the door.

Chapter 27

Fort Collins, Colorado

The snow was heavier in Fort Collins than in Denver. The two cities were only about 65 miles apart, but the air was colder and drier here, as well. Driving north of Route 25 to Fort Collins, Pope had been surprised by the number of vehicles heading south into the capital. The long string of cars proved the phenomenon of suburban sprawl. Fort Collins had become another suburb of Denver.

The Fort Collins Police Headquarters was larger than he expected for a community a sixth the size of Denver. Pope had envisioned the station, and the town, would be more like Mayberry.

Pope checked in with the duty officer and was shown to the Major Crimes offices on the third floor.

"Detective Pope, nice to see you," Detective John Gonzales said with an extended hand.

Pope and his counterpart shook hands.

"Thanks for meeting with me."

"I've been looking forward to it. How's Julian?"

"There's brain swelling. He's still in ICU."

Gonzales shook his head slowly.

"I have some questions regarding Julian's involvement with your case," said Pope.

Gonzales tapped a file in his hand. "Conference room is there," he pointed with the file.

The two men took seats beside one another at the long table. Gonzales spread out the file's contents.

"The investigation was difficult. I was expecting to find a messed-up kid, with inattentive parents, or, worse, abusive parents. But, that's not what I found. The Silers were a family of six. Mother and father, together, and appeared happy. Three girls and one boy. Cody Siler was 14. Two of his sisters were older and one younger. The oldest is in her freshman year at Stanford. Then there's the 16 year-old, who attends the same school as Cody did. The youngest had just turned 8. Family, friends, teachers, all said he was a good kid. Lots of friends. Fit into diverse circles. Not the typical, bullied outsider I expected."

Pope read through a few sheets of interview notes. All corresponded with Gonzales's synopsis.

"Julian made a compelling case for some kind of conspiracy. I mean, four cases and each kid had a pen pal? Can't be a coincidence. Then when Julian found the envelope in the kid's room and we were able to pull the partial fingerprint, I thought we had something. But, the print wasn't in the system."

"So, you believed a middle-aged pervert was twisting kids into school-aged assassins?" Pope asked.

"I don't know." Gonzales shook his head. "Julian made a strong case. And, Cody Siler didn't seem the type to do that kind of thing on his own."

"Parents all over the world say the same thing every day."

"Sure, and I see it all the time. It's always the quiet neighbor, or the kindly uncle, but this really seemed different."

Pope nodded. He laid down the interview notes. "I'm interested in learning your impression of Julian."

"He was dogged. He had spent years working on this angle, and it was proving legitimate. I dare say there was a twinkle in his eye."

"He wasn't rambling or incoherent?"

Gonzales shook his head.

"Paranoid?" pressed Pope.

"No."

"He didn't seem like a man on the verge of a mental break?"

"Absolutely not."

"When was the last time you saw him?" Pope asked.

"Roughly two weeks ago."

Pope nodded. "You saw that the print pulled from the envelope Julian found did not match Addison Ellis."

"Right. I had hoped it would. For the Siler family's sake. For Julian's sake."

"Did the Siler family know Ellis? Was he a family friend or acquaintance?"

"No. I couldn't find a tie to the family at all."

"How about the school, anyone there know Ellis?"

"Nope. I took a photo of your vic to the principal, and he allowed me to show it to Cody's teachers. No one recognized him."

"Did the family recognize the name?"

"Nope. Mrs. Siler mailed the pen pal letters for Cody, and she remembered the name on the envelope as Ernest Post."

Pope arched an eyebrow.

"Don't get excited." Detective Gonzales shook his head. "I checked it out. No matches."

"I meant the name. It doesn't seem strange to you? Ernest Post. Earnest mail."

Detective Gonzales's eyes widened as he nodded his understanding.

"Any chance I could talk to the family?" Pope asked.

"I've already cleared it with them. They want to help Julian, any way they can."

Chapter 28

Denver, Colorado

"Mr. Trope, this is Moina, from the Harvest Moon." She twisted the phone's cord in tight circles around her finger.

"Moina, it is so nice to hear from you! Would you please call me Pearson?"

Moina could feel her face flush. Butterflies fluttered deep within her.

"Pearson, I've found your amulet," her voice cracked.

"You are a gem! Thank you. When can I pick it up?"

"It's not here yet. I just ordered it. Two days . . . I mean, I put a rush on it, and it will be here in, like, two days."

"That's fantastic! That's just in time for my first shoot," responded Trope. He paused. "But, I'll be out of town, for the shoot."

"Where are you filming?"

"Just up in Boulder. But we're starting just before dawn."

"Oh. I'm sorry."

"Wait a minute. I have a great idea. Would you like to be an extra on the set? Actually, come to think of it, there's a role you might be perfect for."

"Really? Acting?"

"Sure. Why not? You could meet a few other students. We help each other out. Play roles in each other's films. You could make a few connections."

"That sounds great!" Moina exclaimed.

"Oh, but do you have to work in the shop? I'll need you for three, maybe four days."

"I have vacation time. I'm sure Ursula won't mind."

"Wonderful! You could bring my lucky charm with you. You might even end up being my lucky charm."

"Yeah . . . I mean, sure, I'll bring it with me."

"Great. I'll send the script and a list of the times and locations that I'll need you over to the shop. If that's okay."

"I'll keep my eye out for them."

"If you don't see them by tomorrow afternoon, or if you have any questions, please call. Call anytime."

"I will."

"This is great! Bye, Moina."

"Bye, Pearson."

It took Moina nearly a minute to unwrap herself from the old phone cord. It took infinitely longer to shed her smile.

Chapter 29

Fort Collins, Colorado

The Siler home was modest, but well maintained. The carport was crowded with bicycles of various sizes and plastic and wooden sleds. A late-model Chevrolet filled the rest of the small space.

Detective Gonzales led Pope around the Chevy and into the laundry room. "Emilio, Stephanie, we are here," he called out as he pushed the door open without knocking.

The family waited in the kitchen for their guests. A pitcher of iced tea and two empty glasses sat on the counter.

Gonzales made introductions.

"Mr. and Mrs. Siler, thank you for speaking with me," Pope began.

"Would you like some iced tea, Detective?" Stephanie Siler asked.

Pope accepted. Then the group took seats around the dining room table.

"How is Pastor Julian?" Emilio inquired.

"Stable, but not out of the woods yet," Pope responded.

Mrs. Siler made the sign of the cross.

"Tell me about your son," Pope prompted.

The couple exchanged glances.

"He's a good boy," Emilio said. "Most parents will tell you the same thing about their child, but with Cody, it's true."

Pope noted that Emilio used the present tense when referring to his dead son.

"He is thoughtful and considerate. He loves his sisters. He takes care of Lizzy, our youngest after school. He's a good boy."

"Did you notice any changes in his behavior during the weeks leading up to the shooting?"

Both parents shook their heads.

"Where'd he get the gun?" Pope leveled his gaze on the father. He already knew the answer.

"It was mine. I had it since I was a boy. I hunted rabbits with my father." Emilio lowered his chin. "I didn't have it locked up. The kids never showed any interest in it. I just didn't . . ." His voice trailed off.

"You kept it loaded?"

His eyes darted up from the table. "No, Sir. It was never loaded."

"But, you had the shells."

The eyes flitted away again. He nodded.

"Tell me about the letters," Pope prompted Mrs. Siler.

"I thought he was writing a pen pal through school. He had me mail his letters weekly. He seemed happy to have a new friend."

Pope noted the mother used the past tense when referring to Cody. "Did he have many friends?"

"My, yes. I took him to a birthday party and saw him playing with several boys. He was a very good basketball player. Some of the boys were on his basketball team. He played with the park league. But, he seemed to get along with the other boys, too."

"Do you remember who the letters were addressed to?"

"Ernest Post. Cody called him Ernie when he spoke of him."

Pope pulled a picture of Addison Ellis from his jacket pocket and passed it across the table.

"Does he look familiar?"

"Detective Gonzales already showed us his picture. And we've seen him on television and in the papers."

"But you'd not seen him before that? At a supermarket or around the school, maybe, or at a basketball game?"

"No."

"Are your daughters at home?"

"Hope and Lizzy are. Joan just went back to school. She's at Stanford University."

"Lizzy's now nine years old, correct?"

"That's right."

"And Hope is seventeen? Detective Gonzales told me she was in the same school as Cody," said Pope.

"Yes."

"May I speak to her?"

The couple exchanged a nervous glance.

"Hope's improved greatly over the past few weeks," Detective Gonzales encouraged the parents. "I think she'll be fine."

Mrs. Siler nodded. She rose from the table and vanished down a hall. She returned with her daughter in tow. Hope was a pretty brunette, with a confident stride and penetrating eyes. She approached Pope and offered her hand.

"Hello, Detective."

"Hi, Hope. It's nice to meet you. Would you care to join us?"

She gave a curt nod and sat down at the table.

"Hope, have you seen this man?" Pope passed Ellis's picture to her.

"That's Addison Ellis," she acknowledged.

"Had you seen Mr. Ellis before? Before his death made it to the news. At school, maybe."

Hope shook her head.

"Did Cody ever mention him to you?"

"No." Her pretty curls bounced on her shoulders.

"Did Cody ever mention Ernie to you?"

"Yes. Often. He said they were friends. Pen pals."

Pope nodded. "Do you know if Cody and Ernie ever met?"

"He never said they did."

"Did he tell you what they wrote about in their letters?"

"Basketball. He said Ernie was a Miami Heat fan, too."

"Don't you think it strange that they didn't email or text?"

"The Internet's for homework only. And, our cellphones are for calling Mom and Dad." Hope looked to her parents.

"Yeah, but you must sneak a text here or there. Right?" Pope leaned in and gave her a sideways grin.

Hope stayed tight-lipped, but her eyes betrayed a hidden fear.

"We ran Cody's cellphone records," Gonzales said. "All numbers were accounted for. Nothing out of the ordinary."

Pope nodded, but held Hope's gaze. She averted her eyes.

"You're not as innocent as you want us to believe, are you, Hope?"

The young girl shifted in her chair.

"Detective?" Mr. Siler spoke up.

Pope looked to the father. "You run a tight ship, Emilio. There are rules, expectations. But, you remember being a teenager, don't you? When you're not thinking about sex, you're figuring out how to screw your parents. Fuck their rules." He slapped the table. "They don't own me. I decide what I can and can't do."

Hope looked at Pope with tears in her eyes.

"Detective Pope, what are you doing?" Gonzales was shocked.

"What are you suggesting, Detective?" Emilio's nose flared in disgust.

"Your daughter's not the goody-two-shoes she's pretending to be. My guess is, none of your children are exactly who you think they are. I've seen it before. You need to open your eyes."

Emilio Siler stood. "That's it! Get out!"

Detective Gonzales stood, as well. He placed a hand on Mr. Siler's shoulder. Pope stayed seated. His eyes never left Hope.

She squirmed.

"Burner cells, right? You buy them with your allowance. Load them with cash. You taught Cody how to beat the system." He slapped the table again. "Right?"

Hope sobbed.

"That's enough, Pope," Gonzales pleaded.

Pope pressed on. "You're not protecting Cody, Hope. In fact, this secret is what killed him. If you would have spoken up earlier, maybe things would be different."

"Oh, God." Hope's head fell into her hands. Her body shook.

Emilio Siler fell into his chair and starred at his daughter. Mrs. Siler broke into tears. Detective Gonzales stood with his mouth agape.

Pope now moved to the young girl's chair. He placed a hand lightly atop her brown curls.

"Hope, do you have his burner cell?" he asked softly.

Her head nodded under his hand.

Chapter 30

Denver, Colorado

Detective Pope had supplied Ursula with stacks of copies of the evidence pulled from Julian's research. She carefully pored over the material, paying close attention to the notes Julian had made within the margins of the pages.

A soft knock sounded on Ursula's office door. She removed her glasses and found Moina standing in the threshold.

"I was wondering if I could take a few days off," the young woman asked.

Ursula was surprised. Moina had accrued weeks' worth of vacation time over the past three years and had never taken as little as a day off.

"Of course you can," Ursula replied. "What days do you have in mind?"

"Tomorrow, Friday, and Saturday."

"That's not much notice."

Moina stepped into the office. She held a stack of papers that were stapled down the margin and rolled tightly within her grip.

"I know, but this is a once-in-a-lifetime opportunity." She held the papers in the air. "This is an amazing script. And, the guy who wrote it, wants me in it."

Moina's smile was captivating. Ursula couldn't remember the girl ever smiling. There was even a twinkle in the one eye that wasn't covered by her long, severe bangs.

"You have a role in that movie?"

"It's just a small role." Moina's smile slipped a bit.

Ursula stood and gave her a warm smile of her own.

"Of course you may have the time off."

Moina's smile returned.

"Tell me about the movie."

"It's a hard-boiled noir. Set in the 1940s or 50s," Moina responded excitedly. "But, it's really about the fall of Satan. It's great. And, I get to play this woman who falls in love with one of Satan's fallen angels. I have a line and everything!"

Ursula smiled. "I'm really happy for you."

"Thanks." Moina recovered. She tempered her smile. "Shooting starts tomorrow. We're filming at the Boulderado. That old staircase is perfect. Pearson has thought of everything."

"Pearson?" Ursula asked.

"Yeah. He came in for a special order. That's how we met. He's the writer and director for the film. He's really talented." Moina blushed.

"Have fun. I believe *break a leg* is the appropriate sentiment." Ursula gently touched the young woman's arm.

Moina flinched slightly and drew away.

"Thanks," she replied. "I'll be back in on Monday."

Ursula bit her lip as she watched her young friend leave her office.

It had been nearly two years now, but the girl's recovery had been slow. Maybe, thought Ursula, this surprise project was just what she needed to shed the remnants of her old life, for good.

Chapter 31

Denver, Colorado

"Climb in," Pope called to his partner through the window of the SUV, parked outside the police station.

Prebys opened the car door and fastened his seatbelt. Pope pulled away from the curb slowly, just as his cellphone rang. He fumbled with the phone and the wheel until he could read the name of the caller.

"Give me a sec," Pope said to his partner. "It's the ex."

Prebys waved a dismissive hand in Pope's direction.

"Hi, Sara. Is everything okay?" Pope asked.

"Yeah, everything's fine. You busy?"

"I'm driving. What is it?"

"I won't take long. Are you still planning on flying in next Friday?"

"Of course. I won't miss Roane's birthday." Pope heard the irritation in his voice.

"I was wondering if Saturday wouldn't be better," she replied.

"What? Why?"

The SUV slid in the wintery slush as Pope changed lanes. The weather had warmed slightly, and the resulting melt made driving conditions worse. When the sun dropped in the next hour, the coming freeze was bound to cause havoc on the roadways.

"I just thought with your new case, maybe you'd be too busy to miss a day of work," Sara offered.

"Bullshit. I'm not missing my daughter's birthday *or* her party, for that matter. Why don't you want me there?"

"That's not it."

Pope heard the hesitation in Sara's voice.

"It's just that there's going to be a lot of people here. You won't get much time with her. I thought maybe . . ."

"You mean your *parents* are going to be there," Pope interrupted, "and you don't want me and your father to face off."

Pope applied the brakes slowly, but the vehicle fishtailed slightly as he entered the ramp onto Route 87. He turned the wheel into the skid with his left hand and straightened the vehicle easily. Prebys grabbed the handle above his window and let out a short breath.

"See! That's exactly what I'm talking about," Sara spat. "Face off? Why's it always have to be like that with you?"

"With *me*? Your dad threatens me every time we're in the same room. I'm coming to my daughter's birthday party. *On* her birthday!" Pope ended the call.

Pope dropped the cellphone into his lap and put both hands back on the wheel.

"Sounds like you two are getting along much better," Prebys quipped after he released the handle.

"Fuck you."

Prebys smiled. "Linda bought Roane a birthday present. Some purple, fuzzy thing. Can you deliver it, or should we ship it?"

Prebys watched his partner stew behind the wheel. "I want it to get there in time for the party, is all. Maybe, I should call Sara's dad. He could deliver it for me."

Pope flashed his partner a look. Prebys's smile was disarming. Pope relaxed his grip on the wheel and smirked.

"See, you're doing so much better with your anger management." Prebys laughed.

Pope shook his head and fought a smile.

They rode quietly for several minutes. Pope decided he wouldn't miss his daughter's birthday, no matter what, no matter *how* this investigation played out.

"So, you said the Siler kid had a burner?" Prebys asked from the passenger's seat.

"Yup, and I found several texts between this mysterious Ernie, Cody, and another kid named Billy Lipton."

"And, just like that, Billy's parents are willing to see us?" Prebys's tone was incredulous.

"Yup. Dad and step-mom. They said they'd be happy to see us."

"You mentioned a basketball connection," Prebys prompted.

"Billy and Cody referred to Ernie as 'Coach' in several of the text messages. They discussed NBA games, some college games, and even a few high school games."

"And, I'm guessing Ernie isn't the name of the Fort Collins High School coach."

"Good guess."

"And Billy went to FCHS, right?"

Pope nodded. "He only recently moved in with his father and step-mother in Centennial. And, both boys did, in fact, play for their school team. J.V. squad."

Pope exited the highway and then coaxed the heavy utility vehicle to stop at the traffic light. The wheels were having trouble gaining purchase. The navigation system pointed them south, toward the quiet streets of Centennial. Pope made a right, and after a second right, Arapahoe High School came into view.

"Do you suppose Julian made a connection between the shootings in Arapahoe High School with Cody Siler's rampage in Caroline's school?" Prebys mused.

"I haven't been through all of PJ's research as of yet."

"Be crazy if we found a buffalo nickel in the evidence."

"This whole case is crazy," Pope countered. "Could some pervert really be twisting kids to kill their classmates?"

"Is that *all* you're worried about? What if we're dealing with a fucking demon?"

"You starting to believe that, Partner?" Pope turned to look at Prebys.

"I . . . don't know. No, not really, I guess. But, you have to admit, it's scary."

Pope thought of Ursula's cautionary warning.

Chapter 32

Denver, Colorado

As soon as she closed, Ursula moved out of her office and spread Pastor Julian's research material across the large sales counter in the back of her store. The falling sun failed to illuminate the space through the skylights above, so she lit the converted gas lamps that towered above the room. The warm light of the maps made reading easier, but they did little to push the shadows from her mind.

Pastor Julian's handwritten notes in the margins confirmed his quest to identify Bateleur. Ursula knew the character from her understanding of tarot, but Julian was using the title to name his antagonist.

For the second time since being drawn into this case, Ursula reflected on her knowledge of Bateleur. Historically, he was a magician, a sleight-of-hand artist, or a street performer. But Julian, she reviewed in her mind, was only interested in the image of Bateleur as pictured in the Tarot of Marseilles, one of the standard patterns for tarot cards. In that image of Le Bateleur, the performer wears a wide-brimmed hat and stands before a table of games. The image, Ursula knew, is full of symbolism. The brim of the hat resembles a lemniscate, or the symbol for infinity, and the items on the table symbolize the classical elements of earth, air, fire, and water. Bateleur's hands point to the ground and toward the sky, and this symbolizes his ability to span the distance between heaven and earth.

The pastor's notes also referenced the Bateleur cipher, but Ursula's research failed to discover any source material for the supposed cryptic code. Julian usually mentioned the Folger Shakespeare's book of magic alongside the cipher, but her combing of the online digital copy of the grimoire proved futile. Bateleur was not mentioned in the enigmatic tome. Ursula made a note to request copies of the newly discovered pages of the grimoire to see if they could help make sense of Julian's studies.

Within the research materials, Ursula found newspaper articles and numerous printouts from webpages Julian had browsed. All were seemingly unrelated. Julian had researched numerous recent school shootings from across the country. But he also had delved into child murders in England that dated from the nineteenth century.

In 1861, two-year-old George Burgess was murdered by two older boys, Peter Barrett and James Bradley, who were both eight years of age. The case was well documented and terribly disturbing. The two older boys beat and drowned the younger child in a stream in their impoverished Stockport, Cheshire, home in England. The boys admitted their guilt with little remorse, were found guilty by a court of law, and remanded to a reformatory school for five years. Julian had circled a line in the coroner's report: "being moved and seduced by the instigation of the Devil."

Julian's material regarding the Revolutionary United Front, or RUF, was possibly even more unsettling, due to the sheer number of victims. Sam Bockarie's Small Boys Unit and the atrocities they performed during the Sierra Leone Civil War were particularly troubling. The eight-year-old boys of the SBU weren't just soldiers but fiercely obedient, maniacal henchmen bending to their master's corrupted whim. During the war-crimes trials of several ranking officers within the RUF, Bockarie, who was known as "Mosquito," was often ascribed as the devil.

Had Julian believed Ellis to be his Bateleur? Did he believe this Bateleur, this jinni, had whispered into the ears of those children, causing them to kill other children and conduct unspeakable war crimes?

Did he believe that same magician worked his evil charms on Brandon McKay and turned him into Caroline's killer?

And did Julian believe this Bateleur was whispering still?

Ursula shivered while considering the cold world in which Julian had been living.

Chapter 33

Centennial, Colorado

Billy Lipton sat between his father and step-mother on a red leather couch. Detectives Pope and Prebys sat across from them in the immense great room. The house was twice as large as the Siler home, and the two families were dramatically different. Yet, their sons had communicated often.

"Billy, how well did you know Cody Siler?" Prebys asked.

Billy shrugged.

"You texted him several times a week for months."

Billy's jaw tightened, but he did not respond. His eyes were stuck to the coffee table separating him from his inquisitors. His leg bounced incessantly.

"The Heat won last night. Did you watch the game?" Pope asked.

Billy's eyes shot up, and his leg fell still.

"Did you watch it with Coach?" Pope pressed.

His eyes narrowed.

"Who's Coach?" Billy's father, William, asked.

"When was the last time you heard from Coach?"

The boy's nostrils flared at the question.

"Did he like Cody better than you?" Pope leaned toward the boy.

"Cody was a punk!" Billy spit out. "He should have picked a better time. I would have . . ."

"That's enough!" William Lipton stood.

"Punk or not, Coach chose Cody."

"He should have picked me!" Billy screamed.

"Not another word," William said. "Detectives, we're done. You need to leave."

Pope broke his gaze from the teenager and looked up at the father.

"That would be a mistake, Mr. Lipton. Your son had prior knowledge of the shooting. He's in deep. Too deep. I could help him, but he needs to talk."

William considered Pope's response. He looked to his son still seething on the couch. His wife looked at him with tears in her eyes.

"What do you need, Detective?" he asked as he sat down heavily.

Pope looked to the boy.

"Billy, have you been in contact with Coach since the shooting?" Pope lowered his voice.

The boy's leg began to bounce again.

"Did he throw you away after? Is that why you resent him?"

Tears threatened to spill. Billy closed his eyes and looked to the floor.

"You need to answer these men's questions, son," William prompted.

"We need to find this guy," Prebys interjected.

Billy shook his head but never looked up.

"We have a picture of him," Pope whispered across the table.

Billy's leg fell still.

Pope could feel his partner's eyes on him.

"It's hard for a giant like Coach to hide for long."

Billy's head shot up. His eyes were wide.

Pope grinned and nodded.

Chapter 34

Boulder, Colorado

Moina twisted her wrist in the light. The thin scar had vanished under the makeup.

"Don't worry, it won't show."

Moina nodded.

"When you're ready, come on out." Sabrina, the makeup artist, gave Moina a sympathetic smile as she left the trailer.

Moina was embarrassed. She had cried. Big, fat tears had fallen. She hadn't cried in front of anyone since she was eleven years old. She had even allowed Sabrina to hold her as she balled like a baby. All because of some makeup, a hairdo, and a new dress.

Moina stood alone in the movie trailer Pearson had rented for makeup and wardrobe. She admired herself in the long, wide mirror.

Sabrina had started with hair extensions, bringing Moina's razor-cut pixie to a full, thick, shoulder-length do. Then she rolled sections of Moina's new hair onto wide rollers. Next Sabrina gave her a new face. Acne scars vanished. Cheek bones appeared. And, Moina's eyes lit up behind smoky lines and gray shadows. The engine-red lipstick gave Moina's mouth a perpetual pucker. The makeup was overstated and theatrical, and the change was stunning.

Moina gazed at her reflection in the mirror and admired the final product. Her thick hair was sculpted into deep, soft, sloping waves. It was nearly as tailored as her dress. She wore a full-length, white skirt with a provocative thigh split. A belted waist accentuated a figure she didn't realize existed. The white top, with its black side panels, peaked over shoulder pads that enhanced the hourglass illusion. Moina traced the bottom of the tunic-style top with her red fingernails. The V-shape hem flared slightly. Sabrina had called it a peplum, whatever that meant. Moina looked like a 1940s starlet.

But, it wasn't how she looked that caused the tears to fall. It was how she felt. She felt beautiful.

A knock sounded on the trailer door.

"Are you decent?" Pearson asked.

"Come in," Moina replied. She nervously clicked her nails and twisted her fingers together.

Pearson stepped inside. His smile fell into a gape. His wide eyes traced Moina's body. She shivered under his gaze.

"You . . . You look beautiful."

Moina squirmed.

"I *knew* you were right for this part."

Moina's eyes reluctantly met Pearson's. He was smiling broadly.

"It's the hair and makeup. And, this dress." She spun slightly, so that the skirt bellowed.

"No. It's you." Pearson nodded slowly. "It's just you."

Moina raised her chin and fought off another torrent.

"Shall we make a movie?" she asked.

"Absolutely," Pearson replied and pushed open the trailer door.

Chapter 35

Denver, Colorado

"Detective, it is nice to see you," Ursula said when Pope entered her office.

"Where's your friend?" Pope hitched a thumb toward the sales counter.

"She's filming a movie."

"A movie? I didn't know she was an actress." Pope took a seat in the empty chair beside Ursula.

"A friend of hers is filming in Boulder. She has a minor role. She's very excited."

"Interesting." Pope slid the chair closer to Ursula's work station. He pulled a copy of the surveillance tape still from his case folder and handed it to her. "Ever see this man?"

Ursula studied the image carefully. "I do not believe so."

"Ever see the name Peter Rota or Pat Otterson in your paperwork?"

"I will check."

"Thank you."

"Who is he?"

"I found a kid who positively identified this man as a conspirator to a school shooting. He was using the alias Otterson at the time. Then the son of a bitch walked into our precinct masquerading as a lawyer."

"This man looks incredibly tall compared to the officer behind the counter," Ursula added.

"He's nearly eight feet tall."

"And, he just walked out?"

Pope, embarrassed, nodded slowly. "What did you find?" He pointed to the copies of evidence he had delivered to her and then removed his notepad from his jacket pocket.

Ursula spread out the fourteen sheets on the desk. On a yellow legal tablet, in beautiful script, she had made a few notes.

"These pages are from a sixteenth-century grimoire," Ursula began. "In fact, they nearly complete the grimoire found at the Folger Shakespeare Library in Washington, D.C."

"I don't understand. Why would a Shakespeare library want it?"

"The library decided it would like a book of magic like the one found in *The Tempest*."

"I don't remember that poem."

Ursula grinned. "It was a play. Prospero, the main character, is a sorcerer. He uses grimoires, or books of magic, to conjure and manipulate. You should read it."

"I'll make a note." Pope smiled.

"So, these pages are from the Folger's grimoire. They are written in a coded text, but I was able to decipher the code. It was fairly straightforward. The majority of the entries are protection spells."

"Protection from what?"

"Hexes, curses, illness, and demons."

"Demons? It keeps circling back to demons."

"Yes. But, it wasn't the subject matter I found most interesting. The coded portions, the overwriting, is in contemporary ink. The original script was written with iron gall ink. See how the ink is brown." She pointed to an area of one page written in Middle English.

Pope nodded.

"These scanned copies show the color variations nicely. The coded portions in the margins, in a more modern ink, are black. It's as if a modern writer was reusing the original sheets for his own notes."

"Julian didn't have much time with these pages," Pope considered. "Do you think he wrote the coded insertions?"

Ursula shrugged. "I could not be certain, but I would say no. I would guess the author was someone writing in the nineteenth century. His writing is more . . ."

"Like yours? Formal. Wordy."

Ursula grinned and put a hand on her chest. "Well, I never," she mocked.

Pope smiled. He made a note to have the handwriting analyzed.

"The fact the writing is coded also leads me to believe it is not contemporary. The author believed it necessary to hide his, or her, interest in the occult from prying eyes," Ursula added.

"Makes sense." Pope slid a little closer to the copy of the pages. "Okay, but what's it say? Why did Julian fly to New York and assault a woman over this?"

"I do not know, Detective. There is nothing extraordinary about the text on these pages."

"Nothing?" Pope studied the pages for a moment more. "Then, what do these tell you?"

Pope withdrew another stack of photocopies from the case file and handed them to Ursula. She flipped through the copies of the tarot cards Julian had left behind in Erica Lyall's hotel room. When she reached the letter addressed to Thomas Jefferson, Ursula paused. She read the letter carefully several times. Pope watched her with growing interest.

"Do you know what you have here, Detective? This is an extremely important piece of history. There are only seven known letters between President Jefferson and Maria Cosway. This is remarkable."

"I read what I could find on Cosway and Jefferson on the internet. Their relationship is fairly well documented. The fact that she was married adds to Jefferson's reputation as a philanderer. But, why was Julian interested in them?"

"The extent of Jefferson's and Maria Cosway's relationship is unknown. However, the language used between the two in the extant letters does point to a true love affair. This letter discusses Maria's pilgrimage through France. She had given birth to a daughter just before leaving England. It's believed Maria abandoned her husband and newborn because she was suffering from postnatal depression. Sadly, her daughter died while she was abroad."

Ursula paused and sipped from a steaming teacup.

"But, I would say it is Richard Cosway, Maria's husband, in whom Rev. Thomas was interested," she continued.

"Cosway was an artist," Pope offered.

"Correct, but he was also an occultist."

"Okay." Pope pointed to the letter. "The letter mentions a stop in Aubenas, France. Apparently, there was an item there Richard wanted Maria to sketch for him. Any idea what that was?"

"I'm not familiar with Aubenas. I have no idea, Detective."

"Okay. I'll run that down. What about the tarot cards?"

Ursula flipped through the photocopies once more. "This is a standard Tarot of Marseilles deck of cards. They are in horrible condition, but . . .," she stopped midsentence and examined one of the copies more closely.

"It would appear there are words hidden within the artwork on the face of these cards."

Ursula spent an agonizingly long time examining each card with a large magnifying glass as Pope looked over her shoulder. She listed the hidden words she had found on her tablet. *Forward. Reverse. Up. Down. Left. Right.*

"Forward, reverse, up, down, left, right," Pope recited when she put down her pen. "Does that mean anything to you?" he asked.

"The same as it does to you." Ursula removed her glasses.

"Absolutely nothing," Pope agreed.

"But, the Cosway connection is interesting," Ursula countered.

"How so?"

"Rev. Thomas mentioned him in some of the material recovered from his home. I found a receipt for these tarot cards, in fact. They were labeled as Mercurii tarot cards. That meant little to me, until you supplied the Jefferson letter. Richard Cosway was a member of the secret, magical Society of Mercurii."

"Which means?" Pope asked.

"Most secret societies are not very secret at all," responded Ursula. "But, in fact, the Society of the Mercurii actually *was* a secret group. Very little is known about it."

"What does that do for us?" queried Pope.

"Not much, I fear. But, it is still early. We will continue to scour this material for an answer," Ursula said, with a smile at Pope.

Pope smiled in return and turned to leave, thinking, as he did, how much he was looking forward to seeing her again.

Chapter 36

Boulder, Colorado

Moina stood on the cantilevered stairs of the Boulderado. Tears streamed down her cheeks. She held the pistol out. It quavered in her hand. She pointed it down the stairs at the chest of the man standing on the landing.

"Bunny, don't do this!" the man pleaded with wide eyes visible under his fedora.

The pistol's report echoed throughout the hotel's lobby. The man clenched his chest and fell to his knees.

"I told you, don't call me Bunny."

"Cut!" Pearson called out, "That's a wrap!"

The cast and crew clapped and cheered. The actor raised himself from the stairs and collected his fedora. He looked up to Moina and winked.

A huge smile cracked Moina's face. The tears spilled, but this time they were tears of joy.

Pearson ran up the stairs and clasped the actor on the shoulder. They hugged. Pearson turned and climbed the stairs. The giant lifted Moina from her feet and swung her like a bell.

"You were spectacular! The tears were amazing. And, you delivered that line perfectly."

Moina giggled in the man's embrace.

"You were the perfect Nora Easter. Just perfect. It's as if I wrote the role specifically for you."

The two shared a bellowing laugh.

Pearson set her down. But, Moina still felt as if she were floating. She had never been so happy. She smoothed her dress and adjusted her shoulder pads as she and Pearson descended the stairs to the continuing cheers of the cast and crew. With a flourish, he pulled a handkerchief from the actor's suit pocket, handed it to Moina, and then raised his hands to silence the crowd.

"Everyone, it's a wrap. Thank you for your hard work. This will be a spectacular movie." He started off another round of applause and then raised his hands once more. "And, please, help me welcome Moina to the first day of the rest of her life. She has found her calling!"

The group cheered and applauded.

With tears still rolling down her face, Moina smiled and took in the praise.

Chapter 37

Denver, Colorado

Detective Pope sat in Ursula's office and read the NYC detective's report on PJ's assault of Erica Lyall.

Meanwhile, beside him, Ursula continued her research on the recently auctioned grimoire pages. The copies of the evidence from Julian's case had arrived earlier in the day, and now Pope and Ursula were combing through it together.

Ursula occasionally muttered to herself and jotted notes onto the pad to her right. At one point she remarked about an interesting incantation that she had never before read.

"Julian was desperate to see the grimoire pages," mused Pope. "But once he got his hands on them, he just left them behind," Pope said as he slowly shook his head and then carefully stretched in the small space.

"That *is* interesting." Ursula removed her glasses and rubbed her eyes.

"His victim's testimony says he just left it all behind," said Pope.

"Was he interrupted?" Ursula asked.

"Nope. He gave her his gun and left."

"He had a *gun*?"

"Yeah, but it wasn't even loaded."

"That paints a more favorable picture of your former pastor."

"It does," acknowledged Pope. "And, if he wasn't tied to this murder, he may have skated with a good plea deal."

"If he was not interrupted, then he must have found something of interest among these pages." Ursula mused as she pondered the copies on her desk.

Something clicked in Pope's head. He flipped through the police report again, found the section for which he was looking, and asked, "Did you find a list of cities?"

"Cities?" asked Ursula, confused by the question.

"Roman cities."

"The grimoire is written in Latin and English," Ursula said as replaced her glasses. "There is a Latin word here and there of which I am unfamiliar." She paused as a thought occurred to her and then started quickly flipping through the pages. "But, I *do* remember a short list of Latin words. All of which are unknown to me." She found page 13, placed it in front of Pope, and tapped the list with a long, pale finger.

"Albenate, Leucae, and Corinium. Are these cities?" Pope asked.

"Possibly," Ursula responded as she pulled a laptop out from below her desk.

"A computer?" teased Pope. "Welcome to the twenty-first century, Ms. Deshayes."

"I could not operate a business in this day and age without one, Detective," she said.

Ursula opened the laptop and did a quick web search for the three

Latin words.

"Aubenas, Loches, and Cirencester are the modern equivalents of those Latin names, and all are cities! And, Aubenas is . . ."

"Mentioned in the Jefferson-Cosway letter!" Pope finished her sentence.

Ursula did another web search for the small city in southern France that Cosway had mentioned in his letter and which also appeared in the grimoire. Pope stood to look over her shoulder at the laptop.

Nothing jumped out. There appeared to be no overt connection between Cosway and Aubenas or, for that matter, any of the other cities mentioned on page 13 of the grimoire.

Chapter 38

Boulder, Colorado

Moina draped the dress over the back of the chair in the wardrobe and makeup trailer. She caressed the fabric between her hands. She caught a glimpse of herself in the long mirror. A small smile still pulled at the corners of her mouth. The makeup had been scrubbed off, and she stood in her own clothes, but the hair extensions and big, soft waves were still in place. Maybe she should grow out her hair.

A knock came to the trailer door. Pearson stepped inside.

Moina's smile widened.

"Some of us are going up to Aspen. Want to join us?" Pearson asked. His head nearly scraped the low ceiling.

"Aspen? I don't know."

"I have a place there. It's an impromptu wrap party. You should come."

"The weather's so bad, and it's a long ride. My car will never make it."

"You can ride with me. Or one of the others."

Moina hesitated.

Pearson stepped closer.

"I must have my favorite actress at the wrap party."

His smile was intoxicating.

Moina caught another glimpse of herself in the mirror. That stubborn smile was still there. She nodded to her reflection and then to Pearson.

"I'll go."

"Great. You'll ride with me." Pearson stuck out a hand.

Moina took Pearson's hand and let him lead her from the trailer.

Chapter 39

Denver, Colorado

For more than an hour, Detective Pope and Ursula searched the internet for a connection between Aubenas and Richard or Maria Cosway.

They found several interesting articles regarding the Cosway connection to Thomas Jefferson. There was even a searchable database of letters in the University of Virginia's archive, and the letters turned out to be the direct correspondence between Maria and the former president.

Pope and Ursula then expanded their search to include mentions of demons, jinn, and the occult. They found a tattoo and piercing shop named Demon and Merveilles in Aubenas, but nothing more.

"We're missing something." Pope pushed back into his chair in frustration. "What was PJ looking for?"

"His research seems to head in every direction on the compass," responded Ursula. "I would venture there is a key that will tie everything together, but it has not yet revealed itself to us."

"Either he was crazy, or we are." Pope's jaw was tight and his fists were balled.

"He is having surgery today, is he not?" Ursula asked.

"He is. The brain swelling couldn't be controlled with medication, so they must release the pressure."

"Do they know the cause?"

"Not really, but they discovered that PJ's sodium levels were excessively low."

"Sodium. Hmmm."

"Does that mean something to you?" asked Pope.

"Salt. I find it interesting the pastor's ailment is tied to an essential earth element."

Pope's cellphone rang.

"This is Pope," he answered.

"Detective Pope, this is Detective Gonzales from Fort Collins."

"Detective, what can I do for you?"

"How's Julian?" There was true concern in the detective's voice.

"I'll know more, later today."

"Very good. We'll be praying for him. No luck here with Pat Otterson. No property or tax records. The Siler family doesn't know him."

"Same on this end."

"And, thanks for the Lipton lead. Billy Lipton and his father will be at the station tomorrow."

"Sure, no problem. Thanks for letting me handle that interrogation. Gonzales, I . . ."

"Right. I'll get to my point. Julian's journal. Could I have it transferred? Julian kept notes that could be helpful for my Lipton interrogation. I'd be happy to drive down and . . ."

"What journal?" asked Pope.

"His small, black, leather-wrapped journal. It must have been on him when he was arrested. Julian never let it out of his sight."

"What'd he keep in this journal?"

"Everything. Every note, lead, discovery. It was his case file. I can't believe . . ."

"I'll check into it, Detective." Pope abruptly ended the call.

"Journal?" Ursula asked.

"Yup. I think it may be the key we're looking for, and I think I know where to find it." A flicker of a smile crossed his face. "Want to go to church?"

"Hmmm. That could be fun. Would you like for me to put on my pagan robes and bring my magic wand?"

"If you think it'll help."

Chapter 40

Boulder, Colorado

Moina's eyes ached. The world beyond the windshield of Pearson's Land Rover was just a blur. The snow came down heavily. Visibility could be measured in yards. Her fingernails nearly pierced her palms, and she tightly clenched her fists. Yet, Pearson was relaxed behind the wheel.

He spoke of his travels to England and France, Portugal and Sweden, Italy and even Syria. It was as if he had lived a dozen lives across the globe, while Moina just wanted to get out of Denver. Not that she hated the city, she just hated her life. She dreamed of starting anew in a place where no one knew her or her past.

Her legs pushed into the SUV floorboards as Pearson changed lanes to avoid a creeping vehicle. She held her breath. The big engine pulled them through the collecting snow with ease. Moina exhaled.

"You okay?" Pearson asked.

"Are you? How can you even see?" Moina shifted in her seat.

"I can see. Don't worry. It's not that bad."

"It's *not?*"

Pearson laughed. He used his right hand to reassuringly pat her knee.

She was conflicted. The simple gesture warmed her from within, but she wanted both of his hands on the wheel.

Pearson squeezed her knee.

"How'd you conjure those tears so easily today?" he asked, with both hands back on the wheel.

Moina covered her knee with her palm. She could feel Pearson's warmth where his hand had rested.

"Crying's always been easy for me."

"Oh, my. I'm sorry." Pearson's smiled tightly.

"It's okay. I'm just glad I was finally able to put it to good use."

"You really were amazing today."

"Thanks. Sorry about the reshoot." Moina rubbed her shoulder.

"Don't be silly. Tattoos are easy. A little makeup and we were back in action. Sabrina's a talented makeup artist."

Moina rubbed at the scars on her wrists.

"Yes, she is. I didn't expect my tattoos to show through the dress."

"I'm glad we didn't have to cover up your leading man's tattoos as well. He had some serious ink under that suit," Pearson chuckled.

"Glen has a tattoo?"

"A full sleeve. Shoulder to wrist."

"Really? I wouldn't have pegged him for the type."

"What's your tattoo? If you don't mind my asking."

"A rose."

"You don't seem like a flower type of girl." Pearson sniggered. "Sorry. No offense meant, it's just . . ."

"None taken. I'm *not* that kind of girl. It's a *dead* rose."

"I hate to say it, but that seems more your style." Pearson scrunched his nose and gave a little shrug.

Moina laughed. "You're right, it does suit me."

"Does it have any significance?"

"It signifies the death of the old me. The weak me."

"Good for you. I appreciate those who attempt to reinvent themselves."

Chapter 41

Denver, Colorado

The snow was falling heavily when Pope and Ursula pulled up to the church. The parking lot had not yet been plowed, so footing was treacherous. The detective extended a hand to help Ursula through the ankle-deep snow. She used her free hand to hike her long skirt above the snow. Pope caught sight of a provocative lace stocking peeking out of Ursula's tall, leather shoe. Slipping and leaning on each other, they made it through the blanketed parking lot to the offices of St. Paul's Lutheran and Catholic Community Church.

Pope was surprised to see Mrs. Rinehold still at the desk in the church office. She must be a centenarian by now. She was old when Pope was a boy. The memory of her teaching Sunday school sent a shiver down his spine. Mean people never die.

"Hello, Mrs. Rinehold. Is the pastor in?"

She nodded and adjusted her glasses as she examined Ursula.

"Thank you." Pope struck off in the direction of the pastor's office.

"Not in there," Mrs. Rinehold corrected.

Pope turned. He waited.

Mrs. Rinehold went back to her typing.

"Where is he?"

"The sacristy. That's behind the altar."

"I know where it is. Thank you."

"I wasn't sure you remembered. It's been awhile."

Pope shook his head. He held the door for Ursula. She had a tight smile.

They rounded the building to reach the main doors of the church. Once inside, Pope called out for the pastor. There was no reply. They walked up the aisle to the altar.

There was a strange sound coming from the back of the church. Metal on metal, but there was something else.

"Pastor Charles?" Pope stepped around the chancel and through a door in the apse.

The sound continued, but Pope could make out Charles's voice in prayer, as well. He was speaking in Latin, and Pope could now see that the strange sound was caused by stone chips hitting the floor.

Pope and Ursula stepped into the sacristy. Pastor Charles was standing over the cabinet that held the vestments. He wore a denim shirt, with the sleeves rolled up to his elbows. He was covered in white dust. He was chiseling a large stone block and chanting the Lord's Prayer in Latin, the Paternoster, as he worked.

"Pastor," Pope called out.

Charles spun. His eyes looked wild above the paper respirator. He dropped his mallet.

"Sorry, Pastor. I didn't mean to startle you." Pope picked the tool up from the floor.

Sweat beaded on the large man's face. He breathed rapidly, and the paper covering his mouth and nose crumpled inward with each breath.

"Are you okay?" Pope asked with concern.

Charles nodded slowly and pulled the mask down so it hung around his neck. "Surprised, is all."

"Surprised? You look more frightened."

"You did startle me."

"Of course. But," Pope took in the slab on the cabinet, "there's more to it than that. Right?"

Charles's jaw moved, but no words took hold.

Ursula stepped deeper into the room. Her eyes went wide.

"You're creating a Sator Square!" she exclaimed.

Charles looked from the stone, to Ursula, to Pope. He wiped the sweat from his face, smearing the dust and grime across his bulbous cheeks and chin.

Pope stepped forward and laid the mallet on the cabinet. He examined the gray stone more closely. The pastor had been carving letters within a grid on the stone's surface. The words were not familiar to Pope; he guessed they were Latin. The word *sator* was etched into the stone several times, both horizontally and vertically, forward and in reverse. The center of the grid was incomplete.

"What's a Sator Square?" Pope asked.

As Charles looked dumbfounded at Pope, Ursula answered the question.

"The Sator Square is an ancient word square. The first known example was from Pompeii, but it found its true home among the occultists of Medieval Europe. It is believed to be imbued with powers of magic." Ursula ran her hand over the rough surface as she spoke.

"Pastor, I assume this has something to do with Julian's journal." Pope inclined his chin to meet the taller man's stare.

The pastor's eyes flicked toward the baptismal font in the corner of the room. Pope caught the glance and followed the pastor's gaze.

A black leather journal poked out from the dry basin.

Chapter 42

Near Vail, Colorado

"Have you ever been to Aspen?" Pearson asked after a long silence.

The roads were nearly empty excepting for the snow plows that had passed several times. According to the dashboard clock, they had been on the road for a little more than two hours. It wouldn't be too much longer if the weather did not decline any more.

"No," Moina replied. "I can't afford to play there, and I don't want to work for those people."

Pearson turned to look at her. His brow furrowed.

"If you don't mind me saying, Denver doesn't suit you. It's just, with what I've seen today. Your acting, I mean. And your desire to reinvent yourself. I think you're destined for bigger things. You know?"

Moina smiled. "Maybe."

She watched the furrow vanish and the easy smile return.

"How do you do that?" she asked.

"Do what?"

"Read people so well. So easily."

"It's not hard. I'm just *present*. I pay attention. I listen. People really aren't that mysterious."

"And, in a few days' time, you have me figured out, do you?"

"Not at all. Sure, you put down some crumbs, but I have no idea." Pearson looked over once more. "You intrigue me. That's what I like about you."

Moina smiled. She felt her face flush, but she held his gaze.

Chapter 43

Denver, Colorado

Pope flipped through Julian's journal. In addition to its bound pulp pages, it was stuffed with additional sheets of vellum and parchment. There were incantations, drawings, tables, star charts, and symbols throughout the journal; some of them were in Julian's hand and others appeared to date back decades, if not centuries.

"Julian gave you this?" Pope asked.

"No. He gave it to Father Dominic, but I knew what to do with it." Pastor Charles mopped the sweat from his brow. The paper respirator still hung around his neck.

"You should have given it to me or the other detectives working the case. It's evidence."

"I had to do this first." Pastor Charles looked stern, even resolute.

"And what exactly are you doing?"

"Following Julian's wishes."

"Carving a stone?"

"Julian said if anything was to happen to him, we should follow his instructions at the back of the journal."

Pope flipped to the back cover. There he found an image of the Sator Square and sloppy, handwritten instructions to carve it into stone and set it in the floor of the sanctuary.

"What's this carving supposed to accomplish?"

"It will protect our congregation."

"From what?"

"From Bateleur," Charles responded matter-of-factly.

"Bateleur? Like on the tarot card?" Pope asked.

Charles nodded. "It's what we called him. It fits. Bateleur of the tarot is a shady magician. A street performer. A man pretending to be something he is not. A conman." Charles lowered his voice. "Although, our Bateleur is not a man at all."

"You believe he is a demon?" Ursula asked.

"Julian believed that he was."

"But, you do not?" Ursula pressed.

"I . . . I'm not sure what I believe. But, before Julian was attacked he led us to a church in Aubenas, France. We found a letter there from the abbot, and it discussed the installment of their own Sator Square. After the square was placed, the congregation's troubles ceased." Charles opened his arms and looked down at the dust coating his denim shirt. "I guess I *am* beginning to believe."

Pope tucked Julian's journal under his arm and opened his case file.

"Pastor Charles, do you recognize this man?" He handed the man the photo of Peter Rota, alias Pat Otterson.

"This is Addison Ellis," Charles said, examining the photo. His brow furrowed as he handed the sheet back to the detective.

"This is the man who wanted you to pass a message to Julian about Caroline's school shooting?"

"Yes, but he's dead. Right?"

"Actually, no. And, I believe this is your Bateleur."

Pastor Charles gasped and made the sign of the cross.

Chapter 44

Aspen, Colorado

When Pearson pulled the Range Rover into the lane of his Aspen home, Moina had difficulty hiding her awe.

"It's huge," she said with eyes wide and mouth agape.

Pearson chuckled.

"I mean, it's really very nice," Moina recovered.

"I've not had it long. Wait 'till the storm ends and you can see the view." Pearson drove the SUV into the attached garage.

Moina climbed out of the vehicle and followed Pearson into the house. Lights popped on as they crossed the threshold. Floor-to-ceiling windows soared overhead. Stone, iron work, and wood formed a solid foundation below. Rustic appointments met sophisticated tastes.

Moina followed her host into his kitchen. Considering the size of the room and the fancy appliances, she expected to encounter a famous television chef whipping something up at the immense range.

"Can I get you some coffee?" Pearson asked, pulling a press pot from a cabinet.

"That'd be great."

Pearson filled the basket with coffee grounds. Then, he filled a kettle with water and began heating it on the stove.

His cellphone chimed.

"Hi, Jackson. Nope, we're fine. I'm expecting some additional guests. I think they'll be trickling in over the next hour or so. Thanks, talk tomorrow." He ended the call. "That was my caretaker. He has a little place at the end of the drive."

"Seems like a good gig. I mean," Moina spun around with her arms extended, "wow!"

Pearson smiled.

"You said you haven't had this place long."

"Little over a year. Previous owners were in the wine business. They owned a couple of large wineries in California. You should see the wine room." He added nonchalantly, "It holds something like 500 bottles."

"Five hundred? I couldn't fit that many bottles in my apartment."

"Don't get too excited. It's nearly empty. I don't own a winery," he laughed.

She joined him.

The kettle whistled. Pearson poured the steaming water into the coffee press. Then he retrieved a tablet from the counter. He touched its screen, and the world outside the windows lit up. Moina was drawn to the spectacle.

Landscape lights shone through the falling snow to light the sprawling grounds. Small birch trees were wrapped in festive white lights. An open-air fire pit came into view on a stone observation balcony. Long pathways crawled down the mountainside toward the valley below.

"How much of this is yours?"

"Forty acres."

Moina shook her head.

"Please, don't judge me. Generations before me made good investments. I reap the benefits. This is by far my most extravagant purchase. Ever."

Moina turned to face Pearson.

"These are all just things. I won't judge you because of them." She gave him a tight smile.

He brushed her arm and returned the smile.

"Enjoy the snowfall. I'll get the coffee." He touched the tablet screen again, and the lights inside dimmed.

The night outside came into focus through the glass. It was quite a storm. It looked as if there were a few feet of fresh powder on the mountain. And, this was on top of snow that was already deep, as the year had witnessed record snowfalls, according to the news stations. Moina had not been skiing since she was a child. During happier times. Before her father died. Before her stepfather destroyed her family. Now, she couldn't afford the sport.

Pearson returned with two cups. He handed one to Moina, then pulled his cellphone from his pocket.

"It's a text from Glen. He and Mitchell can't get past Vail. They asked us to wait to preview the scenes until tomorrow." Pearson looked up from the phone. "What do you say?"

"We can wait," Moina said, unable to hide the disappointment.

Pearson shook his head. "Not a chance. I can pretend to be surprised. Can you?"

"Surprise? Surprise is easy. I'm an actress. Remember?" Moina couldn't contain her smile.

"Yes, you are, my dear. Yes, you are."

Chapter 45

Denver, Colorado

Pope and Ursula had moved into the nave. They sat on a pew and reviewed Julian's journal, while Pastor Charles continued his work in the sacristy. The sound of mallet on chisel on stone echoed through the church.

"I don't understand the significance of the Sator Square," Pope admitted.

He held a copy of a photo from Aubenas, France. It showed a perfect Sator Square carved into the church's bell tower.

"It's a talisman. It wards off evil. Many cultures used it on their ceramics to keep evil at bay. Occultists believed they could conjure and then control a variety of spirits with the word square," Ursula explained.

"Yeah, but Julian's journal is *full* of talismans and spells. Why is this one so important?"

"I do not know. And, I am not convinced the journal will divulge that particular secret. After all, it was the final clue in a mystery Julian had been unraveling for years. Pastor Charles only knew it as another mystery, not the solution. But, the Sator Square does solve one of our mysteries."

"Oh, really? Which one?" Pope's frustration was palpable.

"The Sator Square is a palindrome. This matches with the clues we found embedded within Cosway's deck of tarot cards."

"Forward, backward, up, down, left, and right." Pope nodded his understanding.

"Julian was chasing Bateleur through the cipher on Cosway's cards, and that cipher led him to the recently auctioned grimoire pages, and then one of those pages supplied the Sator Square. Your pastor solved his puzzle."

"But, what's it mean?"

"I fear we will only know the solution's significance once Julian recovers."

"*If* he recovers," Pope responded gloomily.

"Any word of the surgery?"

"I received a text from Prebys. Surgery was successful. Now, it's a waiting game. If the pressure abates, he may have a chance." Pope looked to the cross behind the altar.

Superstition or not, Pope said a prayer under his breath for Julian's recovery.

"I do have a better understanding of Julian's Bateleur," said Ursula. "This journal details many cases of mass hysteria throughout history."

She went on to explain.

"Pastor Julian had collected an impressive amount of original source material from troubling times in American and European history. The bulk of the collection was from the Great Witch Craze dating from the fifteenth to the eighteenth centuries. Julian amassed court documents, diaries, letters, and newspaper articles from the witch trials in Massachusetts, Scotland, Germany, Italy, and France. The case involving Goody Pease seemed to most interest Julian."

Ursula handed Pope a copy of a letter she had found within Julian's journal. A letter from Reverend Whitcome to Rev. Cotton Mather, it was the deathbed confession of Goody Pease as witnessed by Whitcome.

Pope began to read.

September the 18th, 1692

Reverend Sir,

I am Writing to acquaint You with the end to our Torment. The Goodwife Pease has Died. And on Her Deathbed She recounted the Final hours. Indeed, Her Final words were, 'Soet is gone.' Soet I took to believe was the poor soul's name for The Black Man. Goodly Pease Said of Her corruption that Rener Post had given Her a Whitish Powder to Set Affliction upon the young Women of our town, making Them to take up Fits. After her Death, Members of our town found the Body of Mr. Post in the Forest near the Porter River. The Men went to find Preston Sears, for He was always in the company of Mr. Post, to question Him of what He knew. Mr. Sears has not been found. The troubles of our Town have passed. The Witches who had not yet been Freed, no longer are Afflicted.

Sir yours in what I may,

Rev J Whitcome

When he had finished, Pope looked up at Ursula, who continued to explain.

"Julian used the historical records to identify the parties mentioned in the letter. Teresa Pease, Rener Post, and Preston Sears were members of the Salem congregation in 1692. Julian's own notations indicated that he suspected Soet was Bateleur and that he had persuaded Rener Post or Teresa Pease to poison the women of Salem.

Julian's notes in the margin of the letter also indicated that he believed he had identified Bateleur's modus operandi: as in the case of the school shootings, Bateleur manipulated the innocent to do harm to other innocents."

Pope starred at Ursula, and she continued.

"The case of Goodwife Pease is similar to that of Margaret Rule, which Cotton Mather also recorded in his *Wonders of the Invisible World*," Ursula said.

"Who's Cotton Mather?" Pope asked. His head was beginning to ache.

"He was a Puritan pastor of significant influence during the Salem Witch Trials. Mather supported the inclusion of spectral evidence in the trials. His prolific writing held great sway over the court."

"You're losing me," Pope cautioned. "What's spectral evidence?"

"Sorry." Ursula smiled tightly. "Spectral evidence is the testimony that a ghost visited the injured at the moment of the injury. So, it allowed for absolutely no alibi, because no matter where in the world the accused was at the time of the attack, his or her spectral figure could have visited the victim."

"So," said Pope slowly, comprehending, "that would be an impossible case for the accused to win."

"Precisely."

Pope shook his head slowly as he considered the seventeenth-century court of public opinion.

"If we can trust Goodwife Pease's account of what happened, then we might very well be dealing with a jinni," Pope said.

"Possibly," Ursula acknowledged.

"Or, is Bateleur immortal? Hoping through the centuries from soul to soul," Pope pondered.

"That is another possibility, if we keep an open mind. But, there is something else supporting the jinn theory."

"What's that?"

"Have you ever heard of the Marid?"

Pope shook his head. He now definitely had a headache.

"The Marid are a category of jinn. In fact, they are considered to be the most powerful of their brethren. Jinn are known to whisper into the minds of men, and they are known to take a physical form," Ursula explained.

"Interesting," Pope said, as he scanned Cotton Mather's reply to the Whitcome letter.

"Indeed. I dare say that it is even *more* interesting when you consider that *marid* means giant in Arabic," Ursula added.

Pope's head spun to see Ursula nodding.

"Detective, I've finished," Pastor Charles had emerged from the sacristy. His mask hung around his neck. Dust coated his hair. His shirt was soaked from sweat. He looked exhausted.

"Pastor, I'm taking Julian's journal with me. I'll log it into evidence," Pope said.

Charles closed his eyes and nodded. He was too tired to resist.

"I won't mention your involvement," Pope added, after seeing the man's exhaustion.

"Thank you, Detective."

Pope tucked the loose pages back into the journal, and then he and Ursula rose from their pew.

"Be careful out there. The storm is the worst I've ever seen," said Pastor Charles.

Pope was pretty sure he wasn't just referring to the weather.

Chapter 46

Aspen, Colorado

"Let me guess, they're not coming, either," Moina said.

Pearson examined his cellphone. He shook his head.

"Sabrina, Dilan, and Tony are stuck in the storm, too." He looked up. "Looks like it's just you and me."

"Can we still review the raw footage and the rough cuts?"

"Of course." Pearson beamed. "Let's go to the movies, my dear."

Pearson collected his leather bag with the film discs and led the way down the stairs to an enormous home theater. The room was complete with five rows of theater seating, a huge screen, and acoustic panels lining the walls and ceiling.

"Let me set this up. You want popcorn?"

"Seriously?" Moina giggled.

"Sure. There's a machine behind you. It's digital. Easy to use. Pop us some corn."

Moina nodded and busied herself with the machine, while Pearson worked behind a wall in a technician booth. The corn popped. Moina dumped the popcorn into a bowl, then she took a seat in the front row. The first scene lit up the screen.

Moina saw herself standing on the Boulderado cherry staircase that cantilevered its way to the leaded, stained-glass ceiling above. Moina had wondered if the beauty of the Boulderado lobby would be lost in the black-and-white film, but the scene belayed her concerns. Seeing herself on screen was surreal. It was like seeing a stranger with her face. Tears came to her eyes at about the same time her character began to cry on the screen.

Moina mouthed the words as her character, Nora, spoke her line. The gunshot made her jump. Then, the scene faded to black.

Pearson laid a hand on Moina's shoulder. She turned and wiped her eyes.

"You were amazing. You look so beautiful, and your delivery was perfect. You *are* Nora Easter. You were made for the role."

"Could we watch it again?" asked Moina.

Pearson took the seat beside Moina. He dipped into the bowl and pulled out a handful of popcorn.

"Of course." Pearson used his free hand to punch the remote and replay the scene.

They watched the scene twice more as they munched on popcorn. Moina cried, smiled, and cried some more.

"Thanks for doing this," Moina said as the scene faded.

"Sure. The others can watch it tomorrow."

"No. Not just that. For casting me. For believing in me. For everything."

He smiled. "I found you. But, I think most importantly, you found yourself."

She leaned across the chair and kissed Pearson on his cheek.

"You're going to make an old man blush."

"You're not that old." She leaned across again and this time kissed him deeply.

Chapter 47

Denver, Colorado

The storm was so severe Pope had difficulty getting Ursula home safely. Once there, she demanded that Pope stay the night.

She lived alone in a late nineteenth-century, Italianate house that was once owned by a newspaper tycoon. It was probably the most majestic house of its kind remaining in Denver, and Pope was impressed with its details. The staircase, railings, trims, window sills, and doors were beautifully crafted and in pristine condition. The house looked original and authentic. It seemed to harken to a time long gone, just like its current owner.

Ursula stoked a fire in the parlor's wide fireplace, while Pope sipped from a glass of sherry she had poured for him. Satisfied with the blaze, Ursula sat across the room from the detective in a satin-covered, high-back chair.

"You mentioned your daughter," Ursula prompted over her sherry glass.

"Roane," Pope nodded. "She's eight years old. She lives with her mom in San Diego."

"That is a wonderful name. It is one not often used these days."

"We named her after my grandmother, who was one of the most beautiful women I have ever known. She was a foster mother to lots of kids, right up until her last days. She died far too young."

"A name is an important talisman. Naming your daughter after her was a beautiful sentiment," Ursula beamed.

"Thanks. I miss Roane, but I think she's doing well."

"Even without her father?"

"Precisely because I'm not there." Pope fortified himself with more sherry. "I had some . . . problems when I returned from Afghanistan. I ignored it. Tried to move on. Sara got pregnant, so we married. I poured myself into my job. Earned my gold badge quickly. I thought I was OK." Pope's face went slack as he stared into the fire and then continued.

"I caught a case that twisted me up. I brought it home. Shut Sara out. I was angry all of the time. I withdrew from her and Roane. Sara called me out on it one night, and all the anger I had shoved down boiled over." He paused. "I pushed her. She hit the floor pretty hard. I didn't . . . would never . . ."

Ursula cradled the small sherry glass in her slender hands and leaned forward in her chair. Pope held his glass to his lips, seemingly alone in the room.

"Have you since been able to deal with the underlying root to your pain?" she asked.

Pope ceased his musing. His mouth formed a slight smile. "I got some counseling, and my doc was able to help me through it." His brow furrowed. "But, I think I've lost my daughter."

"I find that hard to believe, Detective."

Pope shrugged, but found her words comforting.

They sat in silence for a moment. The firelight cast dancing shadows across the room as they sipped their sherry. Watching the flames,

Pope forced his thoughts to return to the present.

"What do the Latin words in the Sator Square actually mean? Can they be translated?" Pope asked.

"Yes, and no. Four of the five words can be translated. Arepo is the enigma. It is a hapax legomenon, which basically means that it appears nowhere else in the known written record. Most scholars believe it is a proper noun, a name. So, one accepted translation is, 'The farmer Arepo works the wheel' or 'holds the wheel.' But, Latin is an interesting language. One word might have multiple translations depending upon the sentence structure and intended context."

"So, you're saying, no one really knows what it means," Pope cut to the chase.

"Essentially, yes," Ursula shrugged.

They sat in silence for a few moments more. Then Pope rubbed his neck and yawned.

"Well, with that, I think it's time to call it a night." He stood.

"Everything is ready for you in the first bedroom off the stairs, on your left. The fireplace should have dispelled the chill from the room by now." Ursula rose from her chair. "Good night, Detective."

"Call me Oren. Good night. Thanks for keeping me out of the storm."

Ursula nodded.

Pope climbed the wooden stairs and found the bedroom. Ursula was right; it was warm and toasty.

He closed the door and switched on the glass-shaded lamp above the antique roll-top desk near the fireplace. He opened Julian's journal and poured over the bizarre world within. The more Pope read, the less he believed Julian was delusional. The facts were adding up, as extraordinary as they were, and the pieces fell into place.

Through tales of witches and the Black Man, Julian had tracked

Bateleur across Europe to England, Scotland, and, finally, the United States. Earlier in the evening, Ursula had explained the Black Man was a euphemism for Satan during the Middle Ages. But, she said, the Black Man could just as easily be a demon or a marid in regards to the witch hunts.

Pope flipped to the back cover of the journal and again stared at the Sator Square. Five words written into a five-by-five grid: sator, arepo, tenet, opera, and rotas. *Could this really be the answer Julian was looking for?*

Pope rubbed his eyes, which were dry from the fire. His mind was clouded, but something about the word square fixated his attention. He was missing a clue, he was sure of it. Something Ursula had said downstairs echoed in his subconscious. "A name is an important talisman," she had said. He didn't know why, but . . .

Wait! That's it! A name!

Pope quickly rifled through the journal to find the Salem letter again. On a clean sheet of paper he wrote the names it contained: Soet, Teresa Pease, Rener Post, and Preston Sears. He compared the list of names with the Sator Square.

Each of the names could be assembled from the letters within the word square.

Pope pulled out his case file and rapidly flipped through the stack of papers. A business card fell to the floor. Pope bent and picked it up. It was the card for Peter Rota, the lawyer who did not exist. Pope placed the card next to the handwritten word square. Like the other names, this one was also represented by the letters in the square. Pope added the name to his list. Below Rota, he added Pat Otterson, the supposed basketball coach; that name, too, was represented in the word square.

Pope dropped his pen and ran a hand through his hair. This wasn't just a list of aliases. According to Julian's research, Pease, Post, and Sears were historical figures, real people. *So, how could each of their names be part of an ancient word square? What did this mean?*

A wave of exhaustion suddenly hit Pope. He raked the coals to let the fire die, took off his clothes, and climbed into bed.

Sleep came more quickly than it had in days.

Chapter 48

Aspen, Colorado

Moina lay on her stomach. The crumpled sheets were gathered at her feet. Some of her extensions had come loose and were splayed across the pillow. Next to her, Pearson leaned on an elbow. His finger gently traced the bent, thorny stem of her tattoo that started just above her left hip and curved up to the oxidized petals on her right shoulder.

"Until now, I've never been a fan of tattoos."

Moina's face was smooshed against the mattress. She smiled awkwardly.

His fingers slowly slid down her spine to the small of her back, causing her skin to prickle. He traced the single, red-black petal that was seemingly caught in the wedge that formed just above her buttocks.

"It's really well executed. A real work of art."

Moina lifted her head to respond.

"Ursula designed it." She arched her back and propped herself up on her forearms. "The name change. The tattoo. Redesigning myself. Ursula, like, inspired all of it. She had a similar childhood. That's why we connected." She gave him a tight smile. "You should see her tattoo. It's huge."

"I like yours." Pearson traced the rose tattoo from shoulder to buttock once more.

Moina moaned, and her back flexed as his finger continued to follow the contours of her body.

"It was bad, huh? The life you're trying to put behind you."

"You've seen the scars."

"I'm sorry."

She closed her eyes and pushed her face into the sheets.

Pearson continued to gently run his finger across her back in small circular motions. Moina relaxed; the tension slipped away under his touch. She leveraged herself so she could speak.

"My stepfather was a real asshole. Ex-military. He never touched me, but he made my life hell. Emotionally abusive. Demeaning. Nothing was ever good enough for him. My mother and I were his slaves. But that didn't bring Mom and me together. Somehow, she blamed me. I felt worthless."

Moina shifted a bit. "So, when I turned eighteen, I got out on my own. Got a job, changed my name, and got the tattoo. Started fresh and tried to put it all behind me."

Pearson leaned over and kissed her on the forehead.

"It still creeps in, now and then," he suggested. "The self-doubt, I mean."

Moina gave Pearson a weak smile.

"Maybe we could get matching tattoos. You know, to commemorate our new lives together," said Pearson.

Moina's eyes went wide.

"Sorry. That was too presumptuous," Pearson backpedaled. He

blushed.

Moina laughed, and then Pearson joined her.

"I appreciate the sentiment," Moina replied.

She inclined her chin, and they kissed. Sex the second time was both tender and passionate.

Chapter 49

Denver, Colorado

Pope awoke to the aroma of coffee. He quickly dressed in yesterday's clothes, grabbed his files, and made his way down the stairs to the kitchen at the back of the old house.

"Good morning."

Ursula was perfectly coiffed, as always. Pope self-consciously smoothed his hair.

"Good morning, Detective . . . I mean, Oren. Did you sleep well?"

Pope stretched. "Like a rock. Thanks for letting me stay."

He placed his files on the kitchen table.

"Looks like roughly another two feet of snow fell last night," she said, nodding toward the window.

"That'll take a while to clear."

"Could I get you some breakfast?" Ursula asked.

"Just some coffee. Thanks."

She poured coffee from an antique percolator into a tiny china cup and set it before Pope.

"I saw the light under your door last night. Any breakthroughs?"

"Maybe. At least, I think it's more than a coincidence. But, I don't see how it will help."

Ursula raised an eyebrow. "What did you find?"

"Multiple names involved in this case and in Julian's historical evidence can be found on the Sator Square."

"Interesting," Ursula slowly said. "May I see?"

Pope spread out the files. He tapped the name list he created the night before.

"Peter Rota was the guy who claimed to be Julian's lawyer. He's the tall guy in the security-camera footage I showed you. Pat Otterson is the basketball coach who was involved with the Siler boy. Rota and Otterson are, we now know, one in the same. The other names are from Julian's research into the witch trials."

"I remember the names from the Whitcome letter. And, I would have recognized the surnames from previous research. They were common in seventeenth-century Salem."

"You studied the trials?"

She nodded. "That is how I became interested in the occult."

Ursula picked up the copy of the Sator Square. She located each of the names on it.

"I also did some research last night. Soet is the Old Dutch spelling for soot. The Puritans were obviously tied to Holland, so the alternate spelling should have been expected. I believe soot is a perfectly acceptable alternative for the Black Man. And, now I see that soet is also represented within the word square."

Then, a strange expression spread across her face as she studied the Sator Square.

"What is it? Did I make a mistake?" asked Pope. "It was late . . ."

"No. Your list is correct, it is something else."

Ursula moved to a tall cabinet in the corner and opened the door. She opened the cabinet to reveal a small desk and laptop.

"Clever," Pope said.

"Modern conveniences are tucked neatly into my world." She gave him a smile.

"What are you looking for?"

"Recent billings. A special order." Ursula scrolled down the list of invoices on the screen and highlighted a transaction. She compared the invoice to the square and gasped.

"What is it?" Pope stood and crossed the room.

"One of my customer's names is on the square."

"What? Do you know him? Do you have his address?"

"He is a first-time customer. Pearson Trope. I did not wait on him, Moina took his order. She did record his address."

Ursula stood and retrieved her cellphone from her purse. She punched a few keys and held the phone to her ear.

"She is not answering." Worry tightened her voice.

"Who?" Pope asked, confused.

"Moina, my sales clerk. I told you about the movie in which she has a role. Pearson is the director."

"Where were they shooting?" asked Pope, his own voice now strained.

"At the Boulderado Hotel in Boulder."

Chapter 50

Aspen, Colorado

Moina stirred from slumber to see Pearson watching her.

"I'm sorry. Did I wake you?" Pearson asked, unmoving.

"No. Sorry, I guess I dozed off."

"Yeah, you looked so comfortable."

"Staring at people while they sleep is a bit creepy." Moina supported her head on a bent arm.

"Sorry, it's just that you are so goddamn beautiful."

"Oh, please!" Moina fell back onto the bed.

Pearson leaned over her, supporting his long frame with one arm. Moina breathed in his resinous scent. It was intoxicating.

"No, seriously. I'm old. You're young and beautiful. I just can't believe you're in my bed."

Moina studied him. He seemed so smitten with her. She raised up to meet his lips.

"Okay. Fine. I'm gorgeous, but don't watch me while I sleep. It's weird," she said.

"So, you plan on staying over again?" Pearson gave her a devilish smile.

"Shut up." Moina slapped him playfully.

"Hey, while I was being a creep and watching you sleep," he smiled, "I was wondering if you ever think about taking revenge on your stepfather."

"Frankly, I try not to think about him at all," Moina answered.

"Sure, that's the voice of an adult. But as a child, did you ever want retribution?"

"Of course. I just didn't think I was strong enough. So, I turned the hate inward instead."

Pearson nodded his understanding.

"But, I've moved on. Started anew, you know? I have a job, my own place, and I'm starting to save a little cash." She smiled. "And, I got laid!"

They laughed and kissed playfully.

"Do you like your job?" Pearson asked when he brushed the hair from Moina's eye.

"Yeah, I guess. Ursula's great. The pay's not bad."

"Are you a student of the occult?"

"No more than the job requires."

"But, you believe in the supernatural?"

"Sure. I've dealt with my share of demons and evil." Moina thought of her stepfather and shuddered.

"You mean that figuratively. I meant it literally."

"Wow, heavy conversation for first thing in the morning," she deflected. "I think I might need a shower before we delve into a discussion of my feelings about life, death, and the hereafter." She smiled shyly.

"Of course. Sorry. I'll rustle up some breakfast while you get cleaned up."

Pearson kissed her again and agilely sprang from the bed to don a green robe that was hanging behind the door. He winked at Moina as he left the room. Moina slowly rose and made her way to the adjoining bathroom.

Chapter 51

Denver, Colorado

The manager of the Boulderado explained the filming was complete; he had not seen the cast or crew since the filming wrapped. With a little coaxing, he did confirm that Pearson Trope was the name of the man who rented his hotel for the shoot.

Pope had Prebys check DMV records. The check revealed a driver's license that indicated Trope's height was 7'10". And, the photo was a match for the man who had claimed to be Julian's lawyer. Meanwhile, property records for the man showed multiple listings, but the Boulderado desk attendant remembered the crew discussing Aspen.

Pope asked a clerk to file a warrant for each of Trope's properties in Denver and across the state. But, he decided not to wait for the slow machinations of the court. Pope instinctively knew he must act, now.

An obnoxious, yellow Toyota FJ Cruiser pulled up in front of Ursula's house. Pope pulled on his coat and gathered his files. From the porch, he waved to Prebys, who was waiting in the vehicle. Then he helped Ursula down the stairs and through the path he had made in the snow while awaiting his partner's arrival. Pope opened the door and eyed the vehicle skeptically.

"I'll take the backseat," Pope said to Ursula. "You might have trouble crawling through."

Ursula smiled. She gathered her long skirt in her right hand and a large, brocade bag in her left.

"She's coming with us?" Prebys asked Pope.

"It's her friend. And, her experience may come in handy."

The door closed with a thud.

"Now we have our very own good-witch Glinda," Prebys smirked.

"And good morning to you, too, Detective," Ursula gave Prebys a bemused smile.

"What's in the bag?" Prebys asked.

"Some things that we may need," was her reply.

"Like eye of newt and toe of frog?" Prebys laughed.

"Something a little more practical, Detective." Ursula cradled the big, heavy bag of books in her lap.

"Knock it off, Max!" Pope scolded

"Okay. Sorry." Prebys grinned. "Hey, it was cold last night. How'd you two keep warm in that big ol' drafty house?" Prebys eyed his partner through the rearview mirror.

Ursula shifted uncomfortably. Pope shook his head slowly in mock disgust.

"Have you heard from the Aspen police?" Pope asked, fastening his seat belt.

Prebys pulled the big vehicle into the street. Plows had been hard at work all night, and as a result less than a foot of snow remained in the traffic lanes.

"Not yet. They got hit hard last night. Nearly four feet of snow. This Pearson Trope guy lives out of town. Big estate. Bought it last year. Back roads, and what not." Prebys eased the big SUV onto the expressway ramp. "Still waiting on a warrant. All we got on him right now is practicing law without a license and fraud. Nothing more pressing."

"What about Moina?" Ursula asked.

"She's an adult," said Prebys. "No one's reported her missing, and according to the staff at the Boulderado, she left with Trope of her own accord."

Pope stretched and placed a hand on Ursula's shoulder.

"Aspen police dispatched patrol officers an hour ago," Pope said. "It's just going to take some time to get out there."

"I hope we have time," Ursula prayed.

"With this snow? Time is definitely *not* on our side. And, there's more snow on its way. It's going to take us five or six hours to get there," Prebys replied.

Chapter 52

Aspen, Colorado

Patrol Officers Neil Iles and Mike Atkinson pulled up to the gate outside the Trope estate. Castle Creek Valley Road had been treacherous. Plows had not touched it since early in the storm. The Toyota Highlander had all it could handle navigating the winding descent into the valley. And, it had started to snow again.

A man dressed in insulated khaki overalls came to the gate. He pushed his wide-brimmed hat up to reveal an enormous mustache and craggy, weather-worn face. Iles approached the gate, while Atkinson stood behind the open car door.

"Officers?"

"Is Pearson Trope at home?" Officer Iles asked.

"I'm not sure. He came in late yesterday, but I haven't seen him yet this morning."

"May we come in?"

"Is there a problem?"

"We just need to speak to Mr. Trope."

"I'll call up to the house."

"That's not necessary. We can drive up and knock on his door."

"Do you have a warrant? I'm pretty sure you need one to come onto his property."

"Why the evasion, Mister . . .?"

"Shoot, I'm not trying to be evasive. Call me Jackson." The caretaker pulled his hat from his head and wiped a sleeve across his brow. "I'm sorry. It's just . . . I like this job, and I don't want to give Mr. Trope any reason to fire me."

Iles stepped closer to the gate.

"We're not trying to get you in trouble. We just need your help." The officer produced a photo of Moina and handed it through the gate. "Is this girl with Mr. Trope?"

Jackson studied the photo.

"I'm not sure. He's got somebody with him up there, but I never saw who it was."

"Well, it's important that we find out."

"Is she in some kind of trouble?"

"That's an odd question. Do you think she might be?"

"You wouldn't be looking for her otherwise. Right?"

The two men exchanged a knowing glance.

"It's just that Mr. Trope is a bit . . . I don't know. Let's say odd," Jackson offered.

"All the more reason to let us in."

"Okay. Hold on. I'll open the gate."

Jackson replaced his hat and trudged toward the gatehouse. Iles nodded to his partner as he returned to the car. The gate swung open slowly. The officers pulled the vehicle through. Jackson approached the Highlander. Iles lowered his window.

"Can I ride up with you? I haven't dug my truck out yet." Jackson pointed to his buried, battered Dodge pickup near the small caretaker's building.

Iles nodded.

Jackson slipped into the backseat, and the SUV started up the drive.

Chapter 53

Just outside Frisco, Colorado

Detective Prebys skillfully maneuvered the big SUV on the nearly empty highway. Meanwhile, Ursula updated him about what she and Pope had discovered about Pearson. Numerous cars were abandoned along the shoulders, and several had careened down into the median. In spite of the chaos, Prebys seemed to be enjoying the drive.

He listened quietly as Ursula explained the link between the Sator Square and a number of unexplained calamities that befell children throughout the preceding centuries. She leapfrogged from the current school shootings back to the child soldiers of Sierra Leone, to the child murder in nineteenth-century England, to the witch trials of Massachusetts, to the troubles plaguing a church in Medieval Aubenas, and finally to Pompeii. Ursula explained that a Sator Square could be found carved on churches or other public buildings or inscribed on pottery or amulets in each of the historical locations she mentioned.

"Pompeii? That was like, the first century or something. Right?" Prebys asked as he expertly navigated the big vehicle through the driving snow.

"That's the one," Pope answered.

"You don't think this guy, Trope, is two thousand years old?" Prebys huffed.

"Ursula?" Pope prompted.

"That is unlikely, Detective. A human may be possessed by an evil spirit, but there is nothing in the written record to support such a person having an extended lifespan. Instead, a demon hops from host to host as necessary. Or, it is possible that the demon may return to the netherworld once he is through with his host."

"Written record? You *study* this stuff?" asked Prebys, incredulously.

"In fact, I have several degrees in religious studies. And, I have an extensive personal library," Ursula huffed.

"So," said Pope slowly, "we could arrest Trope, and then the jinni inhabiting his body could just hop to another host?" Pope asked.

"Yes, but it is likely a certain incantation or spell must be spoken."

"OK, but there's a flaw in your theory. That is, if the demon needs a host to survive," Pope said tentatively.

"A flaw?" Ursula turned in her seat to study Pope.

"Didn't most of the Pompeiians die when Vesuvius erupted?"

Ursula shook her head slowly. "That is a common misconception. Not everyone perished that ill-fated day. Pompeii was a town of about 20,000 people. The death toll after Vesuvius erupted was estimated to reach roughly 2,000."

"I stand corrected," Pope acknowledged.

"Seems strange that this immortal shithead could be foiled by simply carving five words into a stone," Prebys commented.

"Spells, incantations, hexes, and curses have existed for millennia, Detective. Shamans, priests, and holy men from all cultures pray or chant. In Christian monasticism, monks recite a lorica, or type of prayer, for protection. The word is derived from Latin, and it is defined as armor." Ursula turned in her seat and caught Pope's eye. "There seems to be a great power captured by those five simple words."

Pope nodded his understanding.

Their vehicle passed a sign signaling Aspen was 120 miles away. Pope's and Prebys's cellphones chimed at the same time, and Pope viewed the message.

"Judge issued the warrant for Trope's arrest."

Chapter 54

Aspen, Colorado

As the Aspen police department Highlander climbed the long drive to the Trope house, a red bar flashed on the vehicle's computer screen. The onboard printer also began to churn.

"Good news, Jackson. You did the right thing letting us in. There's a warrant printing for your boss."

"What'd he do?"

"Let's just say he's not a good guy."

"Is that girl in the picture in danger?"

"I don't think so. Do you think Trope is dangerous?"

"Just a spoiled, rich guy from what I can tell. Family money going way back."

"Do you know if he has any weapons in his home?"

"He has a fancy target rifle. Like they use in the Olympics. Cost more than my truck. It's in a safe upstairs."

The Highlander pulled to a stop in front of the large, wooden doors of the mansion. The two officers exchanged a glance and then stepped from the vehicle.

"I have a key," Jackson called out from the backseat, before the doors closed.

Atkinson nodded to his partner. Iles opened the rear door for Jackson. All three men approached the house. Jackson unzipped his coveralls and dug inside for the key ring.

"Damn coveralls," he cursed.

He stooped awkwardly, with one hand pulling the zippered opening wide and the other disappearing inside.

"Got it," he said triumphantly.

Jackson spun and fired four rounds from his pistol. Two found their mark, and both officers dropped where they stood.

Chapter 55

Aspen, Colorado

Moina stepped from the shower, dried off, and wrapped the towel around her. She looked down at the pile of hair in the trashcan. It was a strange sight. She turned her head left and then right, admiring herself in the mirror. Maybe she would grow her hair out. Or, maybe not. Right now she felt better about herself than ever before. She mussed her short hair and wondered what Pearson would prefer.

"Knock, knock," Pearson said as he nudged the bathroom door open. "Coffee or tea?" He held a mug in each hand. "I didn't know which you preferred."

"Tea, thank you."

"Oolong with mint."

Moina sipped. "Delicious."

Pearson kissed her. "You're welcome. Hungry?"

"A little."

"This trip was spontaneous, so I don't have much in the house. Jackson usually stocks up when he's expecting me."

"I'm easy to please."

"That's not true. I had to work at it." Pearson smiled mischievously.

Moina laughed.

"I saw Jackson out near the garage. I'm going to see if he has anything I can borrow for breakfast. You'll be okay?"

"Of course." She nodded behind her mug. "Don't be long."

They kissed once more. Pearson playfully tugged at her towel.

"I'll be right back."

He started to walk out of the bathroom, but turned.

"Do you have to work this week?"

"Yeah."

"Bummer. I thought maybe we could do some skiing. I think I have some things that would fit you."

Moina smiled.

"I could call Ursula."

"Call her, please." He winked, then ducked out of the room.

A week together. She felt her pulse quicken. She knew they were in the golden hour of a new relationship. They were enamored, smitten, obsessed even, but she didn't care. It had been a long time since she felt this way. The last relationship ended badly, they all ended badly, and this one might not work, either. But, at this moment, she didn't want it to end.

Moina sipped her tea, looked at herself in the mirror, and decided to pursue this for all it was worth.

"Now, where's my phone?" she asked her reflection.

Chapter 56

Outside Aspen

The snow continued to fall, but the big SUV handled the foul weather well. The detectives and Ursula were making good time; they were now less than an hour away from Trope's Aspen home.

As they drove, Ursula consulted the large volume she had brought along. As she read about the inscriptions and graffiti of Pompeii, occasionally she removed a stubby pencil tucked in her fair hair and made a note in the book's margins.

"Interesting," she mumbled.

Pope leaned over the seat. "Find something?"

"The author would like us to believe there were Christians living in Pompeii at the time of its destruction."

"'Go therefore and make disciples of all the nations,'" Pope quoted Matthew 28.

"Yes, but could the disorganized Christian cult have reached the south of Italy in roughly 40 years?"

Pope twisted his face as he weighed the possibility.

"The best argument I have read would tie the proliferation of the cult through the slave trade. A Christian could have been enslaved in the Galilean region and then transported to Pompeii," Ursula extrapolated.

"But," Ursula continued, "the argument suggesting a Christian presence in Pompeii seems to rely too heavily on the paralleled existence of the Sator Square in the Roman town."

"Does she always talk like that?" Prebys asked his partner through the rearview mirror.

Pope smiled. "So, there's a Christian angle to the square?"

"The Latin words *pater noster* can be assembled from the square in the shape of a Greek cross," Ursula responded.

"Our Father?" Pope asked. "But, that doesn't account for all the letters."

"Correct. Four letters remain, two being *a,* and two being *o.* They qualify as the first and last letters of the Greek alphabet, alpha and omega."

"'I am the alpha and the omega, the beginning and the end,'" Pope quoted Revelations.

Ursula nodded.

"But you don't believe the square is of Christian origin," Pope observed.

"I do not. However, I did find something of interest in my reading. There are three known examples of the Sator Square in Pompeii. There is one near the amphitheater, one on the house of a woman called Julia Felix, and a partial square on a residential building now called "the house of Paquius Proculus" due to an election inscription for Proculus near the home's entryway. Many buildings are now named after their graffiti." Ursula waved off the statement as if it needed no further explanation. "Anyway, I found the home interesting not only because of the partial Sator Square, but also because of what else was found in one of the rooms."

Pope leaned in expectantly.

"In a small room to the east of the home's *peristyle*," Ursula paused, "the bodies of seven children were found."

Prebys looked into the rearview mirror and locked eyes with his partner.

"That must be a coincidence. Bodies were found huddled all over the city," Pope countered.

"Possibly," Ursula agreed. "But, the other political inscription on the building's doorway is also intriguing. It denounces the election bid of a man named Sertor Pansa Narses."

"So what?" Prebys furrowed his brow.

Ursula held Pope's gaze. His eyes darted back and forth as he made the connection.

"His name is on the Sator Square." Pope shook his head as he slid back in his seat.

Chapter 57

Aspen, Colorado

Jackson removed his hat and wiped his brow. He squinted against the whirling snow. The storm had moved in and obscured the valley; visibility could be measured in feet. He replaced his hat and bent to scoop another shovel full of snow from where the cops had fallen. He carried the shovel to the edge of the garage and added the red-tinged snow to the pile. He added several more scoops of clean snow to cover the blood.

"Jackson."

Pearson's voice brought him to attention.

"Here, bury this in the snow, as well." He handed Jackson Moina's cellphone. "Where are the bodies?"

"I put them in their car, Sir. It's in the other garage," Jackson answered.

Pearson held a flattened hand over his eyes and peered across the wide lane to the detached garage.

"I wanted to take the snowmobiles," he said.

"I covered the car with a tarp. She won't see them."

"Good." Pearson's gaze fell on Jackson. "We're almost finished here, my friend. Thank you for dealing with our guests."

"I hoped you wouldn't be upset."

"Nonsense. I won't need much longer. You bought me the time I needed." Pearson clasped the man on the shoulder. "Is everything ready at the homestead?"

"Yes, Sir. Just as you requested." Jackson looked up into the storm. "I'd suggest you get out there soon. It's supposed to get worse."

"Thank you. You've done . . ." Pearson hesitated. His eyes narrowed. He pointed to a spot in the driveway. "You missed a spot."

Jackson saw the blood. His pulse quickened.

"Damn. I'm sorry, Sir. I'll attend to it right away."

Jackson threw the cellphone into the pile and then rushed to remove the tinged snow. When he turned back around, Pearson was gone.

Jackson dumped the red snow onto the phone and then covered it all with fresh snow. He leaned the shovel against the garage wall and arched his back. He then looked across the driveway to the canvas-covered police vehicle in the garage. Jackson would have laid down his life for Pearson. But, he had done his job well, so perhaps it would not come to that.

Jackson had so wanted to continue following his master and help with his transition into the new host body. The master's current host frame was nearly eight feet tall. Jackson hoped the girl, the new host, would exude the same power.

But, he had done all he could for now. Jackson straightened his back and listened to the falling snow. All was in order for what was to come next.

Chapter 58

Aspen, Colorado

Moina wedged her hand between the cushions of the theater seats.

"Hey."

Pearson's voice startled her.

"It turns out that Jackson is a coffee-and-cigarettes-for-breakfast kind of guy. Sorry, he didn't even have a couple of eggs." He cocked his head. "Whatcha doing?"

"Looking for my phone. I was going to call Ursula."

"Going to ask for more time off?" Pearson teased.

"Maybe." Moina's smile was equally teasing. "But, I can't find my phone, and I don't know her number without it." She threw up her hands. "I don't know *where* it is."

"It's here somewhere." Pearson crossed the room and took out his cellphone. "Here, call your number."

Moina punched her number into Pearson's phone. She held it to her ear.

"It's ringing." She lowered the phone, listened, and looked around the room. Nothing.

"We'll try again upstairs," Pearson suggested.

"I think I turned the ringer off. I didn't want any distractions while we were watching the movie."

"Don't worry, it'll turn up." He took her hand. "I do have a loaf of frozen bread. What some toast?"

"Sure."

They climbed the stairs to the kitchen. Pearson pulled the bread out of the freezer while Moina used Pearson's phone to leave a message on Harvest Moon's voicemail. She found it strange that Ursula was not in the shop. Then again, if the storm was as severe in Denver as it was in Aspen, Ursula probably couldn't make it through the snow in her old, crappy Accord.

"Hey, I was thinking, after this amazing breakfast," Pearson mocked, "maybe we could take the snowmobiles out for a short ride."

"Snow's a little deep for that, isn't it?"

"There's a place I want you to see. The path is protected by the forest. The snow will be lighter there, and it's not too far."

Moina shrugged.

"It's the property's old homestead house. It dates to 1875 and is still standing. It's really charming."

Moina looked out through the immense windows to the blowing snow.

"Just a short walk from the homestead house are the hot springs. They're rustic, but beautiful. The water bubbles up at just over 100 degrees." Pearson wrapped his arms around himself.

"The best part is, it's so secluded you don't have to wear a suit." He waggled his eyebrows and grinned.

Moina laughed. "Why not? If you think it's safe."

"We'll be just fine." Pearson smiled broadly.

Chapter 59

Aspen, Colorado

The FJ Cruiser pushed and slid through the snow as it descended the backside of Aspen Mountain.

Trope's estate—or was it Bateleur's estate?—came into view. It was an immense structure made of wood, glass, and stone. Positioned on the canyon's edge, it appeared that it slid down the mountain and came to a rest just above the river below.

Pope whistled. "Walking the earth for two thousand years must be profitable," he said from the edge of the SUV's backseat.

Prebys drove slowly to the gate barring their entrance into Trope's property. No one could be seen through the driving snow.

"What do you think?" Prebys asked.

"There's a warrant," Pope replied.

"Yeah, but we don't have a copy."

"I'll try the Aspen police to see if their unit has checked in." Pope pulled his phone from his pocket, but there was no signal in the heavy storm and deep valley.

"There is a snowmobile approaching," Ursula announced.

A figure dressed in insulated overalls and wearing a wide-brimmed hat came into view. He hopped off the snowmobile, opened the gate, and approached the SUV. His hands were visible as he grabbed the fender of the vehicle to make his way to the driver's window. Prebys lowered the window a crack.

"Howdy," Jackson said as he pushed the hat back on his head. "Saw you coming. Hard to hide this thing, even in this storm." He patted the door of the big vehicle.

"We're detectives from Denver. Is Mr. Trope at home?"

"Detectives? Denver, you say." Jackson made an overt motion of checking Ursula out in the passenger seat.

Prebys held up his gold shield to the window.

"Are you here to see the other cops?" Jackson asked.

"There are other officers here?" Prebys and Pope exchanged a glance.

"Yup. Came in a few minutes ago. They're up at the big house." Jackson pointed up the snow-covered lane. "Sorry. I left my machine in your way. Give me a second, and I'll lead you up there." He pulled his hat down tightly and hobbled back through the snow.

"Awfully accommodating for a minion," Prebys said as he eased the big SUV forward.

"Better be careful, Partner," responded Pope. "Something seems off."

Chapter 60

Aspen, Colorado

The property's original homestead was made of logs. It nestled in a group of large aspens and near a stream that steamed in the cold, winter air. The snowmobile ride had been harrowing, but short. On a warm spring day, the walk to the cabin from the main house would have taken less than an hour. Seeing the small, rustic house with its wide porch and stone stairs was well worth the cold, bumpy ride. Moina even paused in the biting wind to admire the little place and its view before joining Pearson inside.

Pearson was lighting a lantern when she entered.

"It's lovely," Moina said as she shook off the snow. Her breath plumed into the cabin. "Ooh, but cold."

"I'll start a fire," Pearson said as he crouched beside the large, stone hearth. "I kept this place rustic. No electricity. No running water. But, I'm now thinking about converting to geothermal. It seems a no-brainer with the springs so close by."

"No. Don't," Moina protested. "Leave it as it is."

Pearson smiled up at her as he lit the starter log and stacked kindling around the gestating flames.

"Do you come out here often?" Moina asked as she squatted next to him.

"Not enough. Jackson comes out and stays a month or two in the fall, but I haven't been here in six months or more."

"I'd move out of that monstrosity up on the ridge and settle down here if I were you. It's . . . perfect," said Moina, watching the fire take hold.

"Why don't you?" Pearson asked as he stood. "I mean, why don't you move out of the city and move in here."

"What?" Moina stood, as well.

"Sure. It's not like I'm asking you to move in with me. Move in here." He opened his arms and turned slightly. "Rent free, of course."

"I couldn't."

"You'd be doing me a favor. You'd keep this place tidy. Jackson can show you how to keep it maintained. It'd be a win-win."

"You're assuming I'd *want* to be a kept woman. I have ambitions. Goals of my own." Moina crossed her arms and tightened her jaw.

Pearson raised his hands defensively. "Oh, no, that's not what I'm suggesting. I didn't mean . . ."

"Relax, relax, I'm kidding!" she laughed.

"You had me," he chortled. "OK, then, you could live here and continue your education, or write a novel, or paint a masterpiece. I could set it up so you could get Internet access, and you could save the world with some kind of charity from here."

"I definitely would *not* want Internet access out here. It would ruin things." Moina looked around the cabin in the glow of the firelight.

"You wouldn't, huh?" Pearson smiled.

"I haven't said yes!"

"Right. Sure." His smile was lopsided. "You want to see the hot springs while this place warms up?"

"Yes, I do."

Pearson extended his hand to Moina. Reaching for it, Moina failed to notice the circle of salt drawn on the floor.

Chapter 61

Aspen, Colorado

Prebys pulled the SUV up to the wide carpark between the opposing garages. An Aspen police vehicle sat in one of the garage bays to the right. Prebys and Ursula waited in front of the FJ Cruiser while Pope crawled out of the back of the vehicle.

Pope adjusted his shoulder holster and jacket as he looked back down the lane to the property's open gate. A chill ran down his spine. He felt the familiar rise of adrenaline in his system, but he just couldn't identify the cause.

"Come on in," Jackson called over the wind. "Mr. Trope's entertaining the other police officers inside."

Pope stared at the Aspen Police Highlander in the garage. There was a set of footprints leading to and away from the vehicle. Pope craned his neck to see deeper into the garage. A tarp was rolled up near the vehicle's front quarter panel. Pope looked back to the lane and saw two sets of snowmobile tracks and their own SUV tracks stretching toward the gate.

"How long ago did the other officers . . ." Pope's question was interrupted by the gun shot and Ursula's shrieking scream.

Chapter 62

Aspen, Colorado

"This is it!" Pearson spread his long arms out over the natural pool just below the mouth of the hot spring.

"Awesome," Moina beamed. "How hot is it?"

"102 degrees just out of the ground. It's about 97 in the pool."

"Wow."

Pearson unzipped and shrugged off his thick, insulated coat. Then he started on the buttons of his shirt.

"Are you serious?" Moina asked.

"Sure. Why not?"

"We're in the middle of a blizzard!"

"Precisely. Warm and toasty and buck-naked in the middle of a blizzard." Pearson pulled of his boots and unzipped his snow pants. "What could be better?"

Moina looked back along the short distance to the homestead.

"Don't worry. You'll be back inside before you even cool off." Pearson now stood naked in front of her.

Moina took in his tall, muscular frame as he quickly stepped into the steaming pool. After only a few steps, he was up to his waist in the hot water. He turned to catch her staring at him.

"It drops off a bit, right . . . about . . . here." Pearson sank to his nipples and then smiled at her. "Well, are you coming in?"

Moina shook her head, but smiled. "I can't believe I'm doing this."

She began to shed her winter gear.

Chapter 63

Aspen, Colorado

Detective Pope dropped to one knee and drew his service pistol from under his jacket. Several shots rang out. A bullet ripped through the FJ Cruiser's hood to Pope's left. Pope raised his weapon and found his target. Jackson was in a shooter's stance in the center of the snow-covered lane. Pope pulled the trigger three times. Jackson was knocked off his feet. Pope kept his gun leveled on the man, but he didn't move.

The snow seemed too bright. Pope's ears rang and his heart echoed off the valley walls. He felt a forgotten bitterness clawing its way through him. Burning away the old scabs. Opening the old scars. Something threatened to swallow him whole, but a scream anchored him to the moment.

Ursula was crying his name. She sat awkwardly in the snow, pressing both hands to her hip. Keeping an eye on the fallen Jackson, Pope held his pistol in both hands and ran in a crouch to her side. Jackson's bullet had caught Ursula in the left side, just below her waist. The pelvis was probably shattered.

"You're going to be okay," Pope reassured her.

He then looked over to his partner. Prebys lay unmoving on his right side. His face was in the snow.

Pope took Ursula's chin in his hand and looked into her eyes. "I'll be right back."

She whimpered.

"I promise. Right back." He forced a smile.

Pope slid over to his partner and checked for a pulse. It was stronger than he expected, but he knew he had to act quickly. He glanced once more at their attacker. There was still no movement. Pope holstered his weapon, grabbed the collar of Prebys's coat, and dragged his partner to the garage bay that held the Aspen police vehicle. Pope opened the Highlander's door and whispered a silent prayer. *Yes!* The keys were in the ignition.

"Ursula, I'll be right there," he called to her.

She was sobbing, but surprisingly calm. Pope worried about shock.

He drew his weapon once more and ran to Jackson's body. He kicked the man's weapon away and then checked him for a pulse. He was elated to feel nothing.

"Fucker!" he whispered before turning his attention back to Ursula.

He crouched beside her and gently pulled her hands away from her wound. He gave her a reassuring smile. Pope was baffled. There was blood, and she was in pain, but not nearly enough. The bullet should have blown straight through her hip. Then, the big, brocade bag lying beside her caught his eye.

"It's not too bad. Your bag slowed the bullet. I know it hurts, but you're going to be okay."

Ursula gave him a strained smile.

"Okay, I have to get you out of the cold. This is going to hurt."

They locked eyes and both nodded slowly.

Pope gathered Ursula in his arms and carried her to the Highlander.

Tears fell from her eyes, she bit her lip, but she didn't cry out.

Pope turned on the Highlander and grabbed the radio handset. Pope told the dispatcher they had officers down at the scene and they needed an ambulance and backup. He then handed Ursula the microphone.

"I have to check on Max. When you hear someone on the other end, simply push the button to respond." Pope gave her his best smile. "You're doing great."

Ursula nodded.

Pope turned his attention to his partner. He found the bullet hole in Prebys's right chest, just below the collarbone. Pope applied pressure to the wound. Prebys's eyes shot open, and he gasped.

"Hey, Partner."

Prebys's eyes were wild but soon focused on Pope.

"GSW. Right chest. Strange angle. You must have turned."

"Shooter?" Prebys asked.

"Down and out," Pope replied.

"Good."

"Backup and a bus are on the way."

"Ursula?"

"She took one in the hip. Her bag slowed the bullet. She'll be okay."

"Trope?"

"No contact."

"Find that son of a bitch." Prebys's eyes were steely.

Chapter 64

Aspen, Colorado

Pearson held Moina in his arms. She wrapped her legs around him tightly. She couldn't touch the bottom. The pool was deep where he stood. The hot water licked at her chin. They kissed passionately. His hands held her buttocks tightly as he supported her buoyed weight.

Giving herself so easily to him was strange for Moina. Trust was not easy, as she never believed she truly would trust another living soul. With Ursula, she had come close, but not even for her could Moina completely drop the veil.

"We should get back inside. I need to check the fire," Pearson said between the kisses.

"Oh, just a little longer," Moina pleaded.

Pearson smiled as she kissed him. "We can continue this inside. Ever made love in front of a fire?"

"No. But, I've never made love in a hot spring, either."

Pearson laughed. "Okay. We can do both, but let's start with the fire. I don't want to burn down a 140- year-old, nationally registered landmark just two years after buying it."

"Fine."

Moina reluctantly let Pearson go and swam toward the edge of the pool. She stretched her foot down to test the depth and slipped under water for an instant. She bobbed back up and stroked once more toward where she had entered the water.

"You should be about there," Pearson called out behind her.

Moina pushed her foot down once more and just brushed the bottom. Something grabbed her foot and pulled her under. She flailed about underwater. The water was dark, so she couldn't see what held her ankle. It felt like a vise. She twisted, expecting Pearson to slip up behind her and pull her free. But, the strong hands that had just held her in a tender embrace never materialized. She breathed in the hot water, and it burned her lungs.

Lights flashed behind her eyes, and then everything went dark.

Chapter 65

Aspen, Colorado

Pope methodically cleared the mansion as fast as he dared. Neither Pearson nor Moina were inside. From the large, wooden deck at the back of the house, Pope saw snowmobile tracks headed into the forest. The driving snow was quickly covering them, but they were still visible. Pope hoped Pearson's head start wasn't too much to overcome.

Pope ran back to the Highlander, past Jackson's body, to check on Max and Ursula. The dead body was being covered by the falling snow. Emergency sirens echoed off the walls of the valley as Pope slid to a stop by his partner.

"There are two dead policemen in the back," Ursula said as she looked over her shoulder into the back seat of the Highlander.

"Trope and Moina are not in the house," Pope replied. "I see tracks in the snow."

"You must find her," Ursula pleaded. She grimaced as she shifted in her seat.

"How you doing, Partner?" Pope asked.

Prebys held his hand to his chest. "Collarbone's broken. Bleeding's not too bad, though."

"You cold?"

"A little."

"Want to risk the pain to get into the car?"

"Ambulance is on its way," Prebys replied.

The echoes made it difficult to tell, but the siren did sound closer.

"You need to follow those tracks," Prebys insisted. "But, don't make a move on the bastard until backup arrives. I'll send the cavalry after you, once they get on scene."

Pope looked toward Jackson's snowmobile.

"Here," Ursula called from the SUV. "These men are wearing winter gear."

Pope opened the rear door and found the two patrolmen splayed across the backseat. Pope struggled to pull the heavy, lined coat from the first man, but relished its warmth as he pulled it on over his sport coat. He would have taken the man's hat as well, but the bullet hole in the forehead caused him to pause. He reached for the hat from the second patrolman.

"Gloves," Ursula said as she retrieved a pair from the passenger's seat.

"You okay?" Pope stood beside Ursula.

"You said I would be, Detective, and I believe you." Ursula handed him the gloves.

"I'll find her," Pope promised as he resolutely pulled on the gloves.

Ursula nodded and smiled weakly.

Pope squeezed her shoulder, then turned and ran to the snowmobile. He cranked the key and throttled the engine. Then he quickly slipped off the driveway and into the deeper snow.

Ursula closed her eyes and found herself praying. Her eyes shot open.

"Rose!" Ursula screamed after Pope's snowmobile.

"What?" Prebys asked.

"Moina! Her name is on the Sator Square." Ursula shifted and screamed in pain and frustration.

"What? No, it's not," Prebys argued.

"Her name's not Moina. It's Rose!" Ursula began to cry.

Chapter 66

Aspen, Colorado

Moina choked and coughed up water. In a spastic motion, she twisted to her side and vomited water onto the worn, wooden floor. She hoarsely coughed and spit. With every breath, a searing pain tore at her chest and throat. Tears clouded her vision.

After several long minutes, Moina sat up painfully and took stock of her surroundings. She was naked, wet, and sitting on the floor in the center of the cabin. She squinted against the pounding in her head and looked around the room. *Where was he? He must have pulled me from the water. He saved me. He must be going for help. Back at the house. Are those sirens?* Moina strained to listen. *He must have called an ambulance.*

She stood shakily and staggered to the mantel, where the fire blazed.

The fire felt wonderful against her skin. She took deep breaths of warm, dry air. The pain subsided considerably. Moina felt, more than heard, the floor creak behind her. She turned as quickly as her pounding head would allow.

Pearson charged at Moina with a knife in his hand, grabbed her by the hair, and jerked her back to the floor.

She struggled against him, but he was too strong. His naked body straddled hers. He held the blade against her throat, and she stopped fighting.

"Tell me you want to live." His voice was thick and wet.

Moina looked into his eyes and didn't recognize the man she saw.

He pushed the tip of the knife into the soft spot just behind her jaw.

"Tell me you want to live!"

"I want to live." Her voice was weak.

"Again," he demanded.

"I want to live," Moina gasped.

Pearson drug the knife along her skin and circled her breast. He grabbed her right wrist in a vise-like grip and squeezed until her fingers splayed widely. The he forced the handle of the knife into her palm and closed his hand around hers.

"Tell me you want to live," he whispered.

Moina was crying and biting her lip.

Pearson stiffened. His eyes darted to the door.

The sound of a snowmobile grew closer. Then, it abruptly stopped.

"Jackson is early," he said.

"Help!" Moina screamed and rekindled her struggle below the giant.

Pearson laughed. "He's not here for you. He's here for me," he sneered.

"No," Moina blubbered as she shook with fear.

"Shh." He licked her tears. "Just tell me, and then I'll take away all your pain."

Her breath was labored, but she held the monster's eyes.

"I . . . want to . . . live." The words bubbled from her lips.

Pearson's eyes narrowed. He snarled as he twisted the knife in her grip, causing the blade to puncture the skin.

The cabin's door flew open.

"Arepo!" Pope yelled.

Pope knew he was right. He remembered PJ's need to find their tormentor's name. He now understood the Sator Square's power. He knew the power of naming your demons. He remembered Jesus asking Legion's name before casting them out.

Pearson stood quickly, jerking Moina off the floor as if she were a ragdoll. He placed her naked body between Pope and himself and shrank behind her.

"I don't appreciate the interruption, Detective." Pearson sounded more animal than man.

"Let the girl go, Arepo!" Pope held his weapon in front of him. "I've got men right behind me. It's over."

"It's never over, Oren Pope," he spit out the words. "I'm eternal. You're dust." Pearson breathed hotly through Moina's hair as he peered around the girl. "Leave, and I'll let you live to dirty another day."

"Not going to happen. I came for the girl."

"As did I!" growled Pearson.

Pope prayed silently as he steadied the gun in his hand.

"I cast you out, Arepo!" He yelled over the howling wind.

"And who do you think you are? Her savior? Her Paul?" Pearson sneered, "No, you are like the seven sons. Be gone, little man, or be destroyed."

Moina shook as she looked down the barrel of Pope's gun. She was ashamed of her nakedness and sickened by her vulnerability. She felt as if she could vomit. Pope's eyes kept roving over her, from her head to her center. *How could he?* She wanted to scream at him. She had to do something. She thought of covering herself with her hands. *Wait! My hand! He is giving me a signal! He is looking at my hand!*

Moina still held the knife Pearson had forced into her hand. She exchanged a knowing look with the detective and adjusted her grip on the hilt. Then she quickly spun and jabbed the blade outward and upward, deeply into Pearson's body.

"I want to live!" she screamed as the knife slipped under the beast's ribcage and found its target.

A powerful gust of wind blew through the open door. Pope staggered and fell to one knee. The giant collapsed, pulling Moina to the floor with him. The fireplace hissed, and the flames leapt. The wind spiraled and rushed out the door, as if the room itself had released its breath. The fire went out in a thunderous clap.

Pope crawled, then righted himself and rushed to the entwined couple. The outside light did little to pierce the darkness in the cabin, but the knife had better luck. Pope looked down his gun into the vacant eyes of the man who had once been Pearson Trope. His finger twitched on the trigger when the lifeless form shifted. But, it was only Moina twisting against the giant's bulk. Pope bent and gently pulled her to her feet.

Moina gasped for air and began to sob. Pope removed his coat, wrapped it around Moina's shaking body, and led her from the dark cabin into the gray light of the winter storm.

Chapter 67

Denver, Colorado

Ursula sat in a long white dressing gown in her parlor and rubbed her left hand over the bandage on her hip. A roaring fire helped to drive the chill of another gray, winter day from her house, but it did little to keep her flesh from prickling as her mind drifted over the events of the last few days. She had not been there for the final conflict, but Moina had described the ease with which Arepo had manipulated her and how close she had come to death. Ursula argued death would have been a solace compared to what Arepo truly had in store for the girl.

Ursula sketched the Sator Square into the first page of a clean Moleskine notebook. The magic square was a talisman against Arepo. There was power in the words. Using hindsight, she was determined to translate the palindrome.

Ursula brushed her hand over the page, smudging the fresh ink of her fountain pen and smearing the last *s* of the square. Below the square, she wrote a commonly accepted translation of the Latin: "The farmer Arepo holds the wheel with effort." Considering Arepo certainly was not a simple farmer, or sower of seeds, as was alternately accepted, she began to assemble her own translation.

Working with her knowledge of Latin, the words took on a more apropos connotation. She scratched her translation below the other: "The begetter Arepo possesses works with the wheel."

"That is as clear as mud," Ursula said to the empty room.

She studied the final word of the magic square, *rota*s, which she had corrupted with the smudge. It now appeared as *rota*. The word sparked a memory. In the margin of the notebook, Ursula wrote Latin Vulgate Bible. Then, from the small, hickory table beside her chair, Ursula retrieved her laptop and searched an online version of the Vulgate Bible for the word *rota*.

The Vulgate was the Catholic Church's official Bible after the ecumenical meeting known as the Council of Trent. A Latin translation of the Bible commissioned much earlier in the fourth century, it pulled from Aramaic, Hebrew, Greek, and other Old Latin texts. As Ursula had not studied this version in some time, she was happy to find an online version.

The search rewarded her with chapter and verse: Psalm 76:19, *vox tonitrui tui in rota*, which translated to, "the voice of Thy thunder in a wheel." Ursula knew Psalm 76 in the Vulgate Bible corresponded to Psalm 77 in more modern versions of the holy book.

She smiled when she read the current translation, "The voice of Thy thunder was in the whirlwind."

Oren had told her of the wind that swirled in the homestead cabin and extinguished the fire after he had killed Pearson Trope.

"So, worked within the wind, did you?" Ursula asked the fire beside her.

A knock came to Ursula's door. She closed the book, retrieved her cane, and awkwardly levered herself out of her chair. She crossed the room and, through the front door's sidelights, saw Moina standing on her porch. Ursula unlatched the door and smiled at her young friend.

"Sorry to make you get up," Moina said as she entered.

"That is quite alright. I am supposed to keep moving so as to quicken my rehabilitation." Ursula closed and relocked the door.

The women slowly made their way to the parlor. Ursula retook her seat while Moina moved to the fire to warm herself.

Ursula self-consciously clutched the neckline of her gown. "Please excuse my appearance. Dressing was too much for me to bear this morning."

"Yeah, I'll bet, considering what you normally wear. This is a nice change." Moina smiled. "I like your hair down."

Ursula returned the smile.

"I came to say goodbye. I'm going to take some time . . . for myself," Moina said as she watched the fire.

"How long will you be gone?"

"I'm not sure. I just need to get away."

"Where will you go?"

"I'm going to drive down to Phoenix, then maybe to the coast."

Moina's expression was stern and unyielding.

"I think it a wonderful idea," said Ursula, forcing a smile. "That is, as long as it's for the right reasons."

"It is." Moina shifted her gaze from the fire to meet Ursula's eyes. "It's like, I'm lucky to be alive, so maybe it's time to start living. Enough is enough." Moina shrugged. "I will never be a victim again. I need to be strong."

"There has always been strength inside you, Moina. Few would still be standing after such an encounter." Tears came to Ursula's eyes.

"Thank you for coming after me," Moina said. "I don't think anybody else would have."

"I only wish we had arrived much sooner. It took us so long to put together all of the pieces."

"I should have known he was too good to be true," said Moina, her voice quavering.

"Honey." Ursula dropped the hand from the gown and stretched it toward her young friend.

Moina reluctantly leaned into Ursula's embrace. They held one another for a long time until a knock startled them.

"Oh. Sorry to interrupt," Pope said from inside the parlor doorway.

"That's okay." Moina released her friend and brushed the hair from her eye.

Ursula gave Pope a tearful smile. "That is why I gave you a key. So, I would not have to rise to meet you at the door every time you decided to check up on me. What has it been, three hours since you last called?"

"I could give these to someone else." Pope walked further into the room with a bouquet of flowers.

"You brought her flowers?" Moina asked.

"What? She doesn't . . . You don't like flowers?" Pope blushed.

"She loves flowers, you boob." Moina shook her head. "I just hope you know what it means to give flowers to a woman like Ursula." Moina raised an eyebrow. "*I* might think it inane, but, trust me, *she* won't."

Pope looked from the flowers to Moina and then to Ursula.

"Oh, Moina." Ursula waved a hand. "Oren, they are lovely. Thank you very much."

"Oren?" Moina groaned. "Oh, jeez. A key. Flowers. And, you're on a first-name basis. This *is* serious."

Pope scratched his head and shifted from one foot to the other.

"I'd better leave you two alone." Moina smiled and shook her head.

Moina quickly kissed Ursula on the top of her head, then left.

"She didn't have to leave," Pope apologized.

"Yes, she did." Ursula wiped away her tears and smiled up at him from her chair. "How is Detective Prebys?"

"Cranky," Pope stepped closer to the fire, "and miserable. So, just about back to normal." Pope smiled.

"I am very glad to hear it."

They both stared at the fire. The events in Aspen played out in the light and shadows of the fire dancing in the hearth.

"Why do you think Arepo left clues for us to follow?" Pope asked. "The nickels, the aliases, and risking a visit to the precinct. He fought like hell, but he toyed with us at the same time."

"Hubris, assuming hubris is not just a human condition. An immortal soul playing in the mortal world would feel like a god among men. His evil was to corrupt and destroy. Those poor children were toys with which he played. He walked the earth for at least 2,000 years, and I believe he must have become cocky." Ursula shrugged.

"Is he really dead?" Pope watched the embers change in the draft. "I mean, can supernatural beings die?"

"One cannot be sure in dealing with such things. But, I believe we are exceedingly lucky. And, I hope we have seen the last of Arepo."

"You know, he . . .," Pope hesitated, "*it* referenced scripture from the Bible. I didn't recognize it at first, but Arepo mentioned the seven sons of Sceva. I think we were dealing with an honest-to-God demon."

"Yes, I recall that story in the book of Acts." Ursula nodded slowly. "That is interesting. But, I think labeling what we have been dealing with is dangerous. We can discuss tradition and folklore, but I do not believe we know exactly what Arepo was. Or," she paused, "is."

Pope turned from the fire and marveled at Ursula's beautiful, white-blond hair. This was the first time he had seen it down. The waves cascaded over her left shoulder. She was awash in white. Her hair, her skin, and the gown seemed to be stitched from the light of a distant moon. She looked radiant. The gown's wide neck revealed more of Ursula than Pope had ever seen. Under his stare, she gathered the garment and closed the gap. They made eye contact.

"Sorry. I was taken by your hair," Pope said sheepishly.

A blush rose from her neckline to her jaw.

"It's lovely." Pope tapped his own right shoulder where he thought he had seen the very edges of something. "Is that a tattoo?"

Ursula held her bottom lip under her teeth as she slid the gown away from her shoulder. Pope could see a rounded wing take shape.

"It is an image of *Callistege mi*, a moth more commonly known as the Mother Shipton. The moth was named after Ursula Southeil, a sixteenth-century witch, because the pattern on its wings is said to resemble her face."

Ursula paused. "My name is a reference to that witch."

"Your parent's named you after a *witch*?" asked Pope, in disbelief.

"I *chose* the name." Ursula rolled her eyes and covered her shoulder.

"Ursula's not your real name?"

"No, *Detective*, it is not."

"Detective?" Pope looked dejected.

"I simply meant . . . never mind." Ursula laughed. "Put those flowers in some water, Oren!"

Chapter 68

Denver, Colorado

"Look who I found out front," Pope called as he wheeled Julian Thomas, sitting in a rented wheelchair, up the aisle of St. Paul's. "He was doing donuts and popping wheelies."

The doctors said Julian's recovery was nothing less than a miracle, but Pope knew there was a little more to it than that.

"I heard the good news," Pastor Charles exclaimed as he met his visitors in the center of the nave.

"All charges were dropped," Pope confirmed.

Charles shook Julian's hand.

"My shrink told NYC's finest I was showing remarkable improvement, but I think my donation of collected grimoires to the Shakespeare Library may have helped tip the scales." Julian shrugged.

"And, the Denver Police?" Charles asked.

"PJ was never charged. A receipt for the knife that killed Addison Ellis was found in the house of Pearson's caretaker, Jackson. He purchased the knife and had the symbols inlaid by a jeweler in Aspen." Pope squeezed his friend's shoulder. "So, we're looking at a free man here."

"How are you feeling?" Pastor Charles asked as he sat down in the pew beside the wheelchair.

"Tired. A few gaps in my memory, but nothing serious. And, I should be back on my feet after a little more rehabilitation."

"Thanks be to God." Charles made the sign of the cross.

"You might want to thank Spider, or Wrench, or whatever his name was," Pope said.

"Who?"

"I think it was Crowbar," Julian replied.

Pastor Charles furrowed his brow in confusion.

"Show him," Pope told Julian.

Julian unzipped his coat and unbuttoned his shirt. Then he pulled the shirt open to expose a Sator Square tattooed over his heart.

"I had it done before I left New York," Julian explained. He buttoned his shirt. "I showed you mine, now show me yours."

Charles smiled and rose from the pew to lead his friend up the aisle.

As they approached the front of the nave, Julian said, "Stop, wait. Is this the spot?" He pointed to the pew beside him.

The three men huddled around the exact place where Father Dominic had been shot and Maddison Willet had taken her own life. A small, bronze plaque had been newly added to the pew that memorialized the two lost souls. Julian took Charles's hand and clasped Pope's around the wheelchair's handle. Pope hesitated, but bowed his head as Julian led them in prayer. Julian squeezed his hand tightly as he finished.

Pope wheeled his friend to the steps at the front of the dais. Set into the floor was the large, stone word square.

"Everyone who takes part in the sacrament stands right here to accept the bread and the wine," Charles said with pride.

"You did well," Julian commended.

"And, this will be enough to protect your congregation?" Pope asked.

"In centuries past, the square has indeed purged communities of Arepo. Its power is obvious." Charles pointed to Julian.

"Sure, but that was at a time of villages in which everyone went to one church. Today we are dealing with metropolises," Pope countered, "in which there are numerous churches serving people of many different faiths."

"True. So, it's our job to spread the word." Charles added, "Many congregations, of all faiths, across the city are now installing their very own squares."

"And, you're forgetting your part in all of this," Julian said to Pope. "You slayed the beast. You thwarted his plans."

"I hope you're right." Pope looked to the stained glass window that depicted a risen Jesus cloaked in white and standing before his unsealed tomb.

Epilogue

Alpine, California

Moina Porter pulled into a gas station in the small California town. Phoenix had been a disappointment. Sure, the weather was great compared to the Denver winter, but she didn't feel at home there. So, she drove south into the Sonoran Desert and then west, following Interstate 8 until she crossed into California. She stopped in any small town that seemed interesting, slept when she was tired, and ate where the food looked good. Her newly found freedom was exhilarating.

After filling her tank, she went into the convenience store to peruse the selection of tasty, plastic-bagged snacks that only resembled food with a cursory glance. *Road snacks were essential to a fulfilling road trip, right?*

Moina dropped her cellophane-wrapped treasures onto the counter, and the cashier immediately started to ring her up without a word. Near the register, hanging from a display rack, were a variety of brightly colored bandanas. She chose a vibrant green one and dropped it beside her cache of snacks.

"How far to San Diego?" Moina asked as he worked.

The attendant looked up, seemingly startled that his customer could speak.

"Thirty to 60 minutes, depending upon the traffic and where you're headed," the cashier replied in a voice much too high for a man his size.

"Seems like a quiet town." Moina brushed the hair from her eye.

"San Diego?"

"No. Here. This town." *You idiot.* "What's its name?"

"Alpine. And yeah, it's pretty quiet, I guess." He checked his register. "That'll be $18.77."

Moina handed him a twenty. "I'm kinda hungry."

The cashier looked at the pile of junk food.

"No, I mean for some *real* food," she clarified. "Any recommendations?"

"Less than a half mile up the road is Alpine Beer Company," he suggested.

"Underage," she replied.

"Oh, really? I would've thought you were older."

"Yeah, I get that a lot."

"Anyway, they have really good food, too."

"Cool." Moina pointed down the street. "Half a mile?"

"Other way," the cashier corrected.

"Thanks." Moina collected her snacks and returned to her car.

She set the bag of high-calorie treats on the front seat and pulled out the bandana. As she was tying it around her hair, Moina saw two street kids walking nearby on the narrow sidewalk. The boy was older and led the way. A girl, who looked really young, followed him. She struggled to keep up and gripped her backpack as if it was all she owned in the world. Moina and the girl exchanged a passing glance. Moina closed the car door and called out. The duo never slowed. Moina jogged to catch up.

"I know you heard me," Moina said as she came alongside the couple.

"Yeah, and we ignored you. Piss off," the boy said.

"I'm not trying to give you a hard time," Moina replied.

"Yeah." The boy stopped. "But, here you are."

The girl nearly collided with her partner. The boy's glare shrunk the girl until her face was no longer visible beneath her tangled hair.

"Sorry. I just wanted to know if you were hungry."

The boy took a step toward Moina.

"There's a restaurant just . . ."

"You looking to score, huh? What you want? Scrips, weed, ice?" the boy interrupted.

"No, I . . ."

"Then why the fuck are you bothering us? Looking for a tag team?" snarled the boy.

"Davis," the girl said. "She's just trying to be nice."

"You shut the hell up. I'm talking to this bitch."

When Davis turned his attention to his friend, Moina struck. She put her thumb under his jawbone and her index finger at the outside corner of his eye, and squeezed with enough pressure to bring the boy to his knee. He tried to talk and pull her hand away, but Moina squeezed more tightly.

"Now, listen," Moina said. "Your friend was right, I was trying to be nice. But, now, I'm not. So, here's how it's going to go." Moina pulled a switchblade from her pocket and opened it with an easy flick of her hand. "I'm going to ask your friend a few questions, and if I don't like the answers, then my blade is going to replace one of my two fingers."

With ease, Moina twisted Davis's head back and forth. The boy's free eye went wide and his nostrils flared.

"OK, then, I'm guessing by your reaction I'm *not* going to like her answers. So, maybe I should save myself the time and just insert my knife now."

Davis whimpered. Moina looked to the young girl and saw a slight smile pulling at the corner of her mouth.

"Or, I could let go and send you on your way."

"Please," the boy muttered.

"Without your friend!" Moina demanded.

Davis' eye took in the girl for an instant.

"What do you say?"

"Okay," Davis agreed.

"I wasn't asking *you*," Moina countered. She looked at the girl. "It's up to you."

The girl met Moina's gaze. She hesitated and then nodded her approval.

"It's your lucky day, Davis." Moina squeezed. "I'll let go, and you'll walk away, without a word. You don't, and it'll be the last worthless thing you ever utter. Got it?"

He tried to nod.

"You can't nod, you idiot. Speak!"

"Okay. I'll walk."

The boy's tears tickled Moina's finger. She released her grip, but continued to hold the blade menacingly. Davis stood. His anger boiled just below the surface. Moina gave him a crooked smile and then casually used the knife to tuck her bangs under the green bandana. Davis trembled before her gaze, raised his hands, and started slowly backing away. He was nearly twenty feet away before he turned his back on them and picked up his pace.

"Sorry about that," Moina apologized as she closed the knife. "You okay?"

The girl nodded.

"What's your name?"

"Serena." The girl's voice was soft and timid.

"Great name. You want some lunch?"

"Yeah."

"Cool. You buying?"

The girl faltered.

"I'm just kidding. It's on me." Moina turned and led Serena up the street. "Ever been to San Diego, Serena?"

"Yeah, we were there a few weeks back."

"I'm going there to visit the daughter of a friend of mine. I could use someone who knows the area. Wanna come?"

"I don't know, I . . ."

"Come on, we girls got to stick together, right? We don't need assholes like Davis." Moina hitched a thumb over her shoulder.

Serena looked behind them. Davis was gone. She took a deep breathe, exhaled audibly, and nodded.

"Right. We'll talk about it over lunch," Moina said.

"Okay. Sounds good." Serena quickened her pace to keep up with Moina. "So, what's your name?"